I0531636

Storylandia

The Wapshott Journal
of Fiction

Issue 42

The Wapshott Press

Storylandia, Issue 42, The Wapshott Journal of Fiction, ISSN 1947-5349, ISBN 978-1-942007-42-5 is published at intervals by the Wapshott Press, now a 501(c)(3) nonprofit, PO Box 31513, Los Angeles, California, 90031-0513, telephone 323-201-7147. All correspondence can be sent to The Wapshott Press, PO Box 31513, LA CA 90031-0513. Visit our website at www.WapshottPress.org to learn more. This work is copyright © 2022 by Storylandia. The Wapshott Journal of Fiction, Los Angeles, California. Copyright © 2000-2022 the authors and are reprinted here with the copyright owners' permission.

Storylandia is always seeking quality original short stories, novelettes, and novellas. Please have a look at our submission guidelines at www.Storylandia.WapshottPress.org or email the editor at editor@wapshottpress.org

Donations happily accepted at www.donate.wapshottpress.org

Cover image "Plums" by Amy Emerald Prindle, www.amyemeraldprindle.com

"Proof of Character" was previously published in the Summer 2020 issue of *The Charleston Anvil*.

Storylandia

The Wapshott Journal of Fiction

Founded in 2009

Issue 42, Summer 2022

Edited by Ginger Mayerson

Contents

Chris Viner

The Visitor

It was hard to believe that only two years ago Carry had been so on the ball that she'd blagged them an Echo Park residence for just over $1500 a month, because these days, she seemed to do nothing but sit on a heap of unwashed clothes and watch re-runs of Friends. Her eyes fixed to the screen, her hands passing out treats to their fattening dog, Picasso. The more her partner of two years watched her grow increasingly apathetic as the months went by, the more he heard the falsettos of Phoebe, and Chandler's darker delivery, the more he wondered what Carry really wanted; specifically, whether she wanted *him,* in any capacity at all. He had thought about posing this question to her but hadn't, since her blasé responses to *all* questions of his, had, at best, seemed insensitive. Thus, his anxieties fossilized; he grew unhappy. An intangible tightness, seemed to envelop their interactions; and following this, to George at least, a very acute sense of disappointment. The oddest thing about the situation, perhaps, was that he couldn't say exactly when they'd changed, only that they had. A reluctance to aid had begun to interfere with his motivations; a mild resentment toward her had gathered inside him, like a few pounds of extra weight; a fat tyre strangling the relationship as a result of Carry—not necessarily avoiding him—but simply not caring for his presence anymore. Despite this, he continued to crave acknowledgement. Of course he did. He loved her. Indeed, his appetite for acknowledgement grew, even as her wonder of him appeared to dispel, to grow more and more distant, as the days grew flatter and darker. His loneliness, then, was the most acute of its kind: the pain of being with someone, apparently, not there at all.

"My friend Malcolm's visiting soon. You knew that right?"

"Um-hmm," Carry murmured, as she slurped on a lemonade.

A peel of canned laughter crashed from the television set.

George knew that he shouldn't complain; that really, comparatively speaking, his life was pretty good. This wrapped around the predicament more snugly than he'd hoped: things weren't so bad; not bad *enough*.

Even as he watched Carry decenter, give in, subsume like a particle into the eternity of a numb, ice pop lifestyle, even as he watched his own life slide into the marginal and the petty, he still had no real reason to do anything about it. Thus, he carried with him—though simultaneously neglected—an insidious spore of dissatisfaction, which toughened over time like a scab hardening unnoticeably into a scar. Indeed, it became a part of him, a trademark, like a funny walk, an off-centre hobble on an otherwise relatively healthy looking young man.

The shape of the house was unusual. Although when George looked at its pale blue protrusions jutting out from the street corner it appeared incongruous, the place still possessed a certain charm, a certain *je ne sais quoi*, as he used to quip with Carry in the early days. The three story residence resembled three boxes carelessly stacked one on top of the other. At the time, the no doubt young architects probably thought they'd designed something incredible, something innovative and symbolic of a new generation. Today, most bystanders who took notice found it marvelously appalling in taste. Nevertheless, George's affection for the awkward little block only strengthened over time. Carry had guessed once that the house had been designed in the year 2000: that slight blip of insanity in the history of human culture and trash—she probably wasn't wrong. On each of the three floors there was a medium sized room. On the basement floor was George's study, comprised of an untidy desk and a grotty Mac in the middle; then a pile of loose shoes beside a washer in the corner. On the first floor was the kitchen/lounge area, where an alcove above a basic stove lay view to a plain, L-shaped green sofa, and a dusty television. In between the ground and first floors, was a tiny bathroom, so small that the shower was too uncomfortable to serve as a respite. On the second floor was the bedroom, where from the window they could climb on to the granite roof and watch the sun descend over the lake and the sepia-veiled city beyond. Upon first moving in that was a frequent avocation of the pair: they'd watch the sun bob down in blissful shimmers under the horizon, the radio humming idyllically in the background as they shared cigarettes and weed. George couldn't recall the last time this had happened.

He thought about it now, scraping the burnt food off the stove. In the beginning there was a closeness, an unconscious harmony between the two. They seemed to occupy the same channel of memory and need without conflict. They'd cook together, play cards; they'd watch all the HBO shows and stream all the art-house films. And after, when they'd critique them excitedly, nobody was shot down—each thought or epiphany was met with positivity and encouragement. In those days, there was no money, but it didn't matter. They had each other: content in their cramped, eccentric house, living day to day.

So, what happened?

Well, it was hard to say; hard to mark exactly where the link had broken; where the unravelling from one another's simple Americanized world had begun to curb. This depressed George, since all there seemed to be now was the opposite: they never agreed on anything; a perpetual buried tension lived between them, even before someone spoke. If George wanted to watch the Sopranos, Carry would put Friends on instead; if Carry wanted Korean noodle soup, George would feel a sudden craving for an In-and-Out burger—animal style. Nothing matched. And their little blue house began to look, more and more these days, like their relationship: fractured, out of date, incongruous.

George opened the laundry machine and scraped the clothes from the cylindrical hole, which always gave him a funny feeling—like touching sandpaper, or eating an ice cream straight out of the freezer. He shuffled the rest of the clothes into the hamper. Rolling the cylinder, he wiggled his hand around the machine, checking for stray cotton. His finger brushed along something silky. He pulled it out and threw it on the hamper: a pair of red, lacy lingerie, rested on a mountain of gym socks and gowns. A relic of a pattern of intimacy and desire faded and out-worn. The red underwear now looked rather humorous in the quotidian daylight of such a sobering activity. Or perhaps it was more that after living with Carry for a longer period, the mystery of sex had gone, and he saw now how the initial perfume enraptured in the low-lit dance between man and woman was actually, in retrospect, stupid and phony. The tricks nature played! What fools we all turned out to be in private!

George picked up the hamper and brought it upstairs. He hadn't the energy to philosophize their relationship any longer; no—he refused to over-think a pair of nickers. He had things to do, photos to send to clients before Malcolm arrived. Of course, it was tonight that Malcolm was coming. George didn't know what to feel. He hadn't seen his old pal from college in a long time. What if he'd changed? If they both had? How would they survive two weeks if they didn't get along? Or worse- if Carry hated him?

George's phone buzzed against his thigh in the pocket of his blue USC sweatpants.

Could you pick up some prawn cocktail chips? And some treats for Choppy while you're out? Thnxxx

He sighed through his nostrils. He didn't *think* she was smoking weed again, but you could never be totally sure with someone like Carry...

When they first met they'd smoked all the time, way before they'd gotten together, back when Carry was just a dreamy friend-crush. Things had been different then: the tension a purple thread weaving itself through the past and the sense of possibility. You just can't get back there once you've seen your partner shaking with a fever, or cursing with explosive diarrhea, George thought to himself.

Why was everything so awful and sad? People implied that once you take the leap, you get something else entirely, a higher form of spiritual companionship. Why hadn't this happened? Things only seemed to have gotten muddier in relation to the hopeful beacon of the early days, which he now saw through an angry, dark prism: the smiles through the bus stop windows, the hot wind on sultry summer nights to the latest cinema screening. Somewhere along the line they had lost contact; a special kind of contact they used to have without thinking much about it, and which seemed now irredeemable.

Perhaps it *was* his fault. He had a habit of saying some very stupid things when frustration got the better of him. Last Wednesday, for example, George had suggested that Carry enquire about work at Creative Dreams, Inc. She had worked there once before, and had been forced to quit, due to the stress it had caused her. She'd never quite recovered. He wasn't sure, in retrospect, why he'd mentioned the possibility of returning. He wanted to believe that he was trying to help her again, or that in perceiving her, day in, day out, as insidiously melting like a marshmallow into the fabric of the sofa, he'd panicked. But deep down he knew the truth was much more sinister, that he'd come to resent her laziness, and that he'd wanted her, for a brief moment, to feel just as he felt: misunderstood—like a burning ornament at a party which nobody sees or cares about.

The suggestion, of course, was met with bitter incredulity. She'd reminded him of how small she'd felt, how powerless; the depression that had set in and never quite alleviated; the endless desperation she'd had to bear each day, with a haunted, sad, far away smile. What was he thinking?

"When you watch several dreams pissed on a day," she'd told him, "you begin to realize how evil the structure behind everything is, how shitty people are. Los Angeles isn't a place where people are free to realize their dreams, it's a place where dreams are captured, exploited and, if you're lucky, monetized by guys in suits and gold shirts. Real dreams are just that: dreams. Ineffable. Invisible. Secret. If they turn into reality they suck. Because reality sucks..."

At that moment, Carry's voice had shaken— she'd broken into tears, and George had truly felt like an evil person. He must have been, logically speaking, to have caused such an earthquake, such a rupture of torment, in someone apparently close to him.

He wrote a reply, oozing with slushy guilt:

Sure hon—whatever you want x

He pressed the heart emoji, before deciding against it. The thing was just so overbearing and ridiculous in an individual message, almost hysterical, or offensive.

Waiting for a reply by the washer, he shoved the pair of red lacy underwear, not without rage, further into the hamper, then shut the washer door. The thwomp of cheap metal against the basin causing a mild shudder. Suddenly an image of sickly third world children, stitching clothes under the tin roof of a run-down factory came to him. Sometimes this would happen. Carry had told George that it was because he was depressed himself and didn't know it, but he wasn't so sure. Flies around their lost bulbous gaze seemed to stare directly at him, through the peep hole of his third eye. He looked over at his space grey Apple MacBook: a photoshop spread of a half-edited luxury Hollywood Hills apartment pinned across the screen. He stared, transfixed on the tiny dots of the pixelated wave crest in the background, through the glass windows of the photograph, and felt a numbness burrow down his right thigh.

It was his phone vibrating again. Probably Carry, he smiled.

The smile subsided, and his stomach tightened, as he read the message:

Meet me in 30 dude. Just landed. Chow! M.

"Shit," George whispered.

As he waited outside arrivals, the hot air bringing the damp blue sky closer to the vacuum of the airport, George saw someone whom vaguely resembled Malcom. A famous person, he thought, maybe. Jonny Depp was too interstellar to be waiting for a taxi alone though, wasn't he? Though this *was* LAX. Perhaps he was preparing for a role which demanded more smirking than usual, a return to boyish charm. He looked again. It could have easily been Depp. The jacket, the beard. The otherworldly delusion. He shuffled a bit closer. He'd recently re-watched that artsy-fartsy vampire movie—what was it called? *Only Lovers Left Alive*, of course. Perhaps the figure was actually the main guy from *that* film. He was thinner, which checked out, a little less rugged than Depp. That made perfect sense. It was the vampire. The cool, shoe-gazey musician sucking blood and chasing heroin for a living. Wow, what a life. George pretended not to look, as he approached. He felt an urge to run back into his Nissan. To switch the air con up full blast, and hide. Maybe even cry. But he didn't. He froze. And sure enough, the picture came into focus. The perpetually humored expression, the cocky Sagittarian swagger all the girls loved—or most probably still love. A combination of elements, which, as they pulled together like a weird magic through the hot, jet-lag infused air, could no longer be mistaken as the composition of Malcolm.

There he was. The old prick. It was like the guy had stopped maturing at age twenty.

Malcolm gripped George by the shoulders with his large, muscular hands, then threw him into his chest, making a bearish noise.

"Man. It is good to fucking see you!" Malcolm said.

George was surprised, slightly triggered even. When was the last time anyone had hugged him with such definition? Such clarity?

"Jesus, it's been a long time!" Malcolm continued. "How fucking long's it been?"

George's throat felt dry, akin to the clean air dragging under the revolving glass doors. For a second, he thought his mouth might fail to move, or that he'd forgotten how to shape it in such a way, so as to form ordinary words.

"I don't know," George said, finally. The excessive measure of sentimentality in his voice, causing Malcolm to raise an eyebrow.

"You look like shit!" The old friend exclaimed.

"Thanks."

"No, man, you really do!" Malcolm sniggered. "Just kiddin'."

He jabbed him in the arm. George had thought that he would have lost his punchiness by now. Dimmed the irrepressible spunkiness. The dogged *where next?* cognition. But he hadn't. And for a sad second, George realized that what he was staring at was an example of a happy person, actually enjoying life. One of the few left in the world, it seemed, who were not only free of depression and anxiety, but had barely considered such things. It was quite incredible, George thought—staring at his long, iridescent jawline—that such people existed, moving through the world and going about their business, as if everything were just fine, as if there was no sadness, neither living in their bodies of the past, nor in the sly, frail climate of the future.

"Hey man, you still with that girl, or..." Malcolm rotated his shoulders, ducking and strafing like a boxer.

George couldn't help but admire his lack of public awareness, his apparent fearlessness.

"Carry?" George asked, squinting. He felt like his voice was quieter than it should have been. Then it dawned on him: when *was* the last time he'd had a conversation? Spoken to another man in a way that wasn't repressed by formal constraints?

He hoped the complexity of his emotions didn't draw themselves too clearly on his face—that would have been unacceptable between two guys—or that if they did, Malcolm was too dumb, or maybe too happy, to notice.

"Yeah, Carry!" Malcolm projected, a couple of young women with roller suitcases by the Uber stand turning to look. "Fuck man—I almost forgot the chick's name!"

"Well, yeah, man. Of course—why would you..."

"Good, man. Good." Malcolm sniffed and looked out into the distance, the crowds fading into taxis and cars like light beams. "I'm so happy I'm finally here. My grandparents were fucking killing me, dude. I'll tell you all about it in the car."

He ran over to the curb and yelled for a taxi, his voice rising above the turbulence.

"Oh, you don't do that here, Malcolm," George protested.

Malcolm responded to his dreary attitude, with a loud, uncontrollable laugh, gripping onto George's arm, squeezing it even, as if this were the only way to stop. "You know, I've missed you, man," he said, still stumbling on his own laughter.

A car seemed to appear out of the night mist; Malcolm ran over to the window. George couldn't hear exactly what his friend was saying. No, it was only a feeling he could gather—a feeling that somehow his bright, positive energy, would make the world, strangers even, start doing things for his friend. He caught his own reflection in the vehicle window for a second. The stray blondish hairs where receding had begun early, the long green anorak that didn't fit him anymore, or even suit him. The deep lines, which were really cracks, around his eyes; a signal that something important was being drained from him too early on in the life cycle of a man.

It looked like Malcolm was getting somewhere, his strong neck pushed through the open window. He'd been talking for longer than necessary, which meant he must have found something in common with the stranger. He turned and looked at George, with a glint in his eye, the hand waving for him to get in the passenger seat. That glint, like a neat, surgical wound in the universe, telling George, that of course—of course it was players like Malcolm for whom the world would open their doors.

When George and Malcolm arrived at the house, Carry was entrenched on the sofa like a fallen decoration, immersed in a Netflix documentary about obesity and American corporations. From the back, George could see her loose, brown hair, still bearing its bright faded flashes, a stain of optimism from a few months prior, when, in a giddy jolt of wonder and joy at having been accepted for the role of junior representative at the creative agency, she had dyed her roots blonde, blooming a flamboyant image of herself into existence.

Before she'd began the job at Creative Dreams, Inc., Carry would stand at the balcony, half-looking at, half-absorbing the twinkling lake in the far distance, under the dark, breezy palm trees. A drone of mosquitos mowing over the lily pads, the hot night tuning the important parts of herself to what had seemed then to be the important parts of the world. Soon, she would be around her kind: artistic, bohemian, a group she could call her own for once. There would be recommendations: strange novels, vinyl, art passed around the office. Though it would be more of a commune, a sacred respite for dreamers just like herself, a place with its face cast against the soullessness of the age, eyes fixed on the white stars in the deep blue sky, which if you just looked at them, were beautiful in their flickering persistence, like a reminder to never forget about the soul.

Instead, she had gotten envelopes, and the joyous task of telling fellow dreamers that they owed the agency another bill. Not to mention a small, odd, aggressive boss. Stiff with unhappiness, draining her, every minute she was on the clock, like swimwear.

True: she'd been naïve, expecting it to be far more than it was. A flaw in her character she'd always dragged around, like a limp. But to suffer for it, in this way, and so much!

Well, she'd told herself that she'd never let that flaw get the better of her ever again. Even if it meant becoming mean, old and bitter like the rest of the world around her.

She was wearing now a long, pink sweater, which meant her reservation had reached peak inwardness, as if a shelter had grown over her like a second skin.

"Hey Carry, I want you to meet someone," George said, the breathiness of his voice causing her to shiver, as if she didn't recognize it. But then as she turned, there he was: smaller seeming, cutting an oddly disappointing shape between the rectangular door frame.

"You forgot the prawn cocktail crisps didn't you?" She snapped. "And the Bonios, you forgot those too didn't you?"

George held a weak glance, like a sad, religious man smiling through his pain, his own self-doubt. He crept toward the sofa, and Malcolm took a seat adjacent to Carry. "I'll get some beers," he mumbled.

She shifted her eyes at Malcolm, absorbing his presence for a moment, then continued to watch television.

"Who are you then?" She said.

"I'm Malcolm, I..."

She smiled involuntarily.

"No, you idiot. I know your name. I mean tell us about yourself." She threw more crisps into her mouth and munched. "You're supposed to be staying in my house for a couple of weeks, aren't you? So tell us something."

"Well, what do you want to know?" He grimaced.

"Oh, I don't know. What do you do? Let's start with that."

George uncapped the tops of three beers in the kitchen, scrapping them off the counter into the bin.

"Well, right now I just travel around."

"That so? No job to speak of?"

"Well, I did. I'm an actor actually. I recently did a commercial..."

"Alright, alright, whatever... You still living with your parents then?"

"Grandparents actually."

"Wow, you're even sadder than I expected.."

They both laughed, and Carry was pleased to hear the stranger understand her dry humour, as if a wall had collapsed between them.

"Are you coming to dinner with us tonight?" Malcolm asked, as George passed them both a beer.

"Um..." Carry took a swig. She looked at George in the eyes. She had declined the invitation earlier in the day, George remembered, as he sat slumped on the side of the couch in his shabby suit studying her, one leg dangling from the arm.

He waited for her response.

"Where are we going then?" She said.

In the Uber on the way to the restaurant, there was an energy between Malcolm and Carry. George kept tapping the window with his index, pointing out the best places to eat and drink. A pleasant gesture, that to Carry was a caustic irritation. She closed her eyes, spinning it to white noise; something she was used to doing by now: training her brain to filter out the nonsense surrounding her. Now that summer had passed, Los Angeles had seen a rare few days of showers. The gentle rain through the streets came trickling like a memory into focus; it was like his voice alone could put the whole world to bed.

Carry hadn't been out to dinner in a while. The Eastern décor under the hood of a rouge tinted lamp, the curiosity of new company, gave her a quiet thrill, a warm glow.

She watched Malcolm between small sips of her *Asahi* beer, as George yammered at his side. The way Malcolm studied the menu like a child. His utter absorption in things. Was this what happiness looked like? He asked about *Pho*; what was in it, where it came from. He asked George about his photography, and tensed his eyelids as he listened to his detailed, pretentious response.

Malcolm, she saw, had retained his wonder. A condition which at first amused, then gradually, horrified her, as under the dim glide of conversation and *bon mi*, she recognized this wonder, as the thing she'd lost a very long time ago.

The thought depressed her.

To think that when they first moved in together her perception of George had been a beautiful, congealed fragment, like stained glass, of a man that was sensitive to the small and the painful; understanding of the nature of desire, which was a mire of security and freedom. Even the way she used to hear his voice was different now; she had heard it once as a frail, almost wild thing, like a bird's. Now the sound she heard coming from him was one of bitterness, a man that not only embodied a middling unhappiness, but actively wanted others to share in it with him. She felt her gaze motion over at George— who was laughing with Malcolm—and her stomach begin to turn with contempt. Every idea he planted now appeared to her as meek; all his angles, his sentences, sharp or spoilt by his own disappointment in himself, and his—*their*—situation.

"Well, Malcolm, we're glad to have you with us..."

Where had this new habit come from? This politician's tone? The phony hand gestures? The smile, as though he'd won a prize. Were they always there?—or was it only now, after she'd witnessed, lived through his bad decisions, that she began to notice them? She knew he was unhappy; that he, in a way, thought of himself as a failure. And so this tone, knowing the inward psychology to be the opposite, made her squirm in the dark with a feeling as stale and cool as a dead fish on a platter. She was in the presence of an impostor. Nothing special. But she wanted special. Didn't she? Or did she?

"We've been looking forward to having you join us for this week and I know that Carry and I, well, we've been in need of a little company lately, or... perhaps another viewpoint. What am I saying... Fuck!... it's *good to fucking see you!* Salute, as we used to say in Boston, hm?"

"Salute!" Malcolm raised his glass, as did Carry, stifling an awkward laugh.

"Tell us. How is home? Boston? Your beloved grandmother? Does she still make that divine coddle?"

"Ah, I think we've heard enough about me," Malcolm looked at Carry. "What about you—I still don't really know enough."

"Don't be daft—I've spoken a lot about Carry," George intervened.

"I suppose—but I'd like to hear from her: what are you doing with your life?"

"Well, right now... nothing."

"Oh, come on... we've got a few things brewing—remember what we discussed?" George said, leaning over the table.

"Like what? The agency?" Carry rolled her eyes.

"The agency?" Malcolm asked. "What's that?"

"The agency, Malcolm, is where dreams go to die," Carry responded, taking a large swig of beer. She gulped and put the bottle down. "Employees too."

"It wasn't that bad," George sighed. "I thought you liked it at first…"

"Don't do this." Said Carry.

"What?"

"This. We've had that conversation…"

"I was only trying to help by getting you that job. I had your best interests at heart, you know that."

Carry shifted her chair away from the table, the legs squeaking against the marble floor.

"Honey?" George whispered, putting his hand on hers.

"I don't have to do this right now. So I won't." She downed the remains of her beer. "Thanks for dinner…" She nodded her head in the visitor's direction, pushed the swinging door, and walked out on to the street.

That night, George spooned behind Carry, feeling the warm body that had once responded to him. He felt now that he could barely touch her, that she found him laughable.

"You didn't have to do that you know." George whispered, the polite tone not matching the sentiment.

"Well neither did you." Carry said, the muscles of her back not moving.

George watched the dark, wine-coloured sky hover between the curtains, the black silhouette of a balcony against the backdrop.

He felt the broad, lonely silence, encroach around him.

"When did you start to hate me?"

"I am trying to sleep," she said slowly, an undertone of frustration in her voice.

Silence spread into the corners of the room, then froze inside of him again.

"I don't hate you," she said, finally. "I just... I can't stand it when you try and make yourself look like a hero. When you know how much damage the agency caused me, how it completely altered my perception of the world, how I had to piece myself back together... it was all such a shock. It was... horrible."

"Do you love me though?" George asked, his weak whisper falling on her shoulder. Carry huffed. She lifted her head and patted her pillow down, she was wide awake now.

"Yes, George. Of course I do; of course I love you," she sighed, gazing out at the balcony, the silhouette of strange lines in the middle distance.

"I love you too," George said, closing his eyes, and gently slipping off into sleep.

As Carry watched the dark sky, she thought she saw a bright shooting star riding across it; a miracle. Yes, for sure a sign that things were okay after all. Good even: it's a miracle just to be alive and not know what's going to happen from one day to the next. A miracle. Yes, a beautiful, precious miracle, she thought, as she felt the vibrations of George's snore brush at her neck, beginning to increase in volume, as the landscape before her darkened, until she could no longer tell the silhouette from the sky.

That morning, when the 11 o clock Los Angeles light came through the curtains and set a fair orange-blue tinge through the middle of the house, Carry, for a brief moment, felt hopeful; a hope mingled with pieces of guilt.

She spent the morning having breakfast with Malcolm.

George had told her to entertain him, in a surprisingly straight forward way. His request was so clear of jealousy, in fact, that Carry had been a little hurt that there was nothing in his tone to suggest that he might be even the slightest bit afraid of leaving her in the company of another man.

"Here's $100," he'd said matter-of-factly, "show him around—maybe the lake, some cafes, some galleries with some modern art, or something. You know. All the usual stuff people do." And with that, he'd kissed her on the cheek and driven off to Lake Arrowhead for the day to undertake his latest photography commission.

So, he was gone. Thank god, Carry thought, placing her hands on the cheap, fake plastic marble of the kitchen counter, and taking a deep breath in and out, her eyes closing.

Over a fried breakfast, she laughed at Malcolm's stories about New York, their college days. She put her fist under her chin and listened as he told her of the cultural differences his parents had suffered being Irish upon first moving to Brooklyn.

By the time breakfast was over, her hope had brightened, and her guilt had deepened. She felt she knew Malcolm, perhaps better than she knew George. She felt a sympathy for his condition; that he had a story that seemed alive; that he brought a lively energy she could chime with effortlessly. He knew something about life and the living. There was a resilient innocence still intact, an innocence unable to be contained or analysed. Still, she wanted to pursue it anyhow, if only to blindly absorb a piece of its resolute charm.

At about 1 o clock, they took a walk through the dusky tones of Griffith park; the pine trees overhead swaying in the breeze.

Carry watched a troupe of people climb the flat ochre hills to the observatory. So many of them. Where did they all come from? Some with boyfriends, girlfriends, some with children, some sad looking, some smiling, some distracted by their phone. Tons of people, all searching for an answer, the next moment of wakefulness. What made her special, or anyone for that matter? Weren't we all as lost as each other? They climbed the hill, resting finally on a bench that overlooked the steep, turquoise valley and the Hollywood sign, its pale, haunted lettering in the far distance.

"Thanks for taking me here," Malcolm smiled. "Really. I'd always wanted to see LA. Learn what it's all about. I can't say I'm any closer, but—thanks all the same."

Carry laughed.

"You don't learn what LA is about. Nobody knows that. You just… watch… wonder. And begin to see that everybody's actually pretty similar, that most dreams look the same." A frown grew on her face, she looked down at her feet on the raw tanned ground.

"Why are you so cynical? I always thought that a dream… I don't know… that it was yours to keep. Even if it never came true. Perhaps more for having never been corrupted into reality—and yet never having disappeared. That way, nobody could ever steal it away from you, or exploit it. You know what I mean?"

"I thought that too… but then, things changed."

"How so?"

"The agency."

"Well you've got to tell me about this mysterious agency now—that's the second time you've mentioned it!"

"It was my old job. Helping folks out. You know. With their dreams, their artistic pursuits or whatever. Well—when you see that the people you try to help aren't as special as they think, you realize that the dream is an illusion. That it isn't anything. On top of that, when you realize your job is to exploit that illusion, which is basically the only thing a lot of people have, you start to understand something about the world that isn't good for anyone to learn."

Carry looked out at the crowds walking up and down the track, like colonies of ants on a sand hill, following the same trail back to their cars.

"Come on," she said. "Let's go down there."

They took a walk by the lake, the shadows of pendulous lime-green trees falling beside them. Malcolm pointed out the various fish weaving below the water. They walked, and they talked, through the trails of the forest, and the dry landscape peppered with succulents and cacti; and Malcolm began to feel that although he didn't quite understand it—that he could perceive the beauty of Los Angeles—that its mysterious, unreachable centre, gave all the separate parts and portals of the city, a special fragrance, an air of something; a mood that was alien, romantic and deeply magical all at once. It made sense to him why movies were produced here; and why so many crazy, ramshackle dreamers found themselves, either by choice or chance, rooted in LA.

Carry told Malcolm more about her story, about the agency and her relationship with George;

about her estranged family in England, and about her brother's mental disabilities. And Malcolm told her about New York, his Irish-immigration story there as a child, how all he'd ever really wanted from life was to live it, and to get the best out of the people he met along the way. That that was always enough for him, would always be enough.

They reached a particularly dense plot of trees, and soon they were back on a sidewalk and out the other side of the forest.

They reached the roadside café and sat in a booth by the boulevard; the sun was coming down now—and the street was a dark blue that never failed to make Carry melancholic and hopeful all at the same time.

"I like this café. I like that they show local artists on the wall. It reminds me of when I was inspired by that kind of thing."

"Well—do you make any art?"

"No."

"You're lying! I can see it!"

"I'm not."

"Lier!—show me!"

"Fine. But if I show you—you can only look for a little and you have to promise not to tell Malcolm."

He promised and she reached into her knapsack, unclipped the buckles, and pulled from the dusty interior a worn, blue leather journal with a tight string bow tied around its middle. She gripped onto it, holding it to her chest defensively.

"I'm serious," she said with a smile, "if you don't follow any of those rules—I'll fucking kill you."

Malcolm closed his eyes and nodded, half-serious, as Carry unwrapped her arms and placed the journal on the table. He picked it up and carefully untied the ribbon. Opening the leather front cover, he began to flick through the pages. They were slightly fearful, anxiety ridden, yet sensual portraits of stark, nervous bodies and haunted expressions. As he turned the pages they seemed to deepen in his hands, the antagonistic, deformed figures scoring themselves into the visually sensitive parts of his mind, not seeming to let go. And he saw her then, perhaps better than she could see herself. It felt to him as though some door had suddenly opened, presenting an ink blotted, scattered apparition of who she really was, beneath the surface, before the door threatened to shut again, as Carry raised her hands to grab the journal from him.

"Okay," she said, "you've had enough. You have to give those back now."

"They're beautiful," Malcolm said.

"Shut up..."

"Just one more moment..."

Malcolm jumped out of his chair and rushed over to whom he could only guess was the café manager. Carry folded her arms and rested her head on them in a flood of painful embarrassment. She closed her eyes tight, waiting for Malcolm to finish talking to whoever he was talking to, for the whole ordeal to be over.

She lifted her head from her arms, and there he was, that boyish grin beaming at her.

"I hate you," she muffled into the side of her sweater.

"I've got you a show. I've spoken to the manager, I showed him your work—he said they're busy until Thursday, but that they can give you a one night show on Friday, your work only."

"You're an asshole," she laughed, pulling her

journal from his grip and throwing it into her bag.

When they walked out from the café-gallery, the roads seemed to be shining under the orange and blue sky, and the fading buzz of traffic across the way sounded less relentless than it had done, just a little more correct, as though, all of a sudden, between the ferocity of life, there was room for something like mercy.

Back at the apartment, Malcolm and Carry were sat on the floor in the living room, clipping various pencil drawings into black frames and screwing things together. An empty bottle of champagne lay at the side, next to a buzzing television showing an episode of Friends.

They heard a thud of a door and George came up the stairs. As he surveyed the messy room, a suspicion began to grip him. A mushy, heady sort of feeling. What exactly were they doing with all this arts and crafts stuff? And why *was* there an empty bottle of champagne next to the two?

"Um, hey?" George said in a low voice, hovering over them.

"George! We…" Carry's face paled, she looked over at Malcolm for an answer, who returned her look. Suddenly, she broke into a nervous cacophony of laughter, placing her hand on her stomach.

"I'm sorry, George," she said, unable to control herself. "But your face! Your face!"

She slumped to the ground, and tears began to draw from her eyes.

"What's going on?" George asked. He took off the green suede jacket he'd bought around the time he'd first started dating Carry, and threw it over the side of the couch.

Malcolm slapped his hands on his thighs and pursed his lips. "Well, I might as well tell you. We're getting an art show together for Carry." He said. "I spoke to the manager at that place by Griffith and he's agreed to show her work this Friday."

The room filled with silence. George's cheeks faded, then crowded with capillaries of blood. Creases furrowed on his forehead, as he tilted his head in quiet astonishment.

"I'm gonna make a cuppa," Malcolm said, standing up. He walked across the carpet mottled with stationary and tools, and filled an empty kettle with a measure of cold water.

Carry began to rise from her cocoon of absurdity. She got up, sat on the couch and switched the channel to a wildlife documentary: images of tigers chasing antelopes reeled across the screen to whispery commentary.

"How was your day?" Carry asked.

"What's he talking about? Art?" George trembled.

"I've been making art for a long time now. I knew you'd get weird about this." Carry was sat cross-legged, she had an air of joyfulness in spite of George, which irked him. She had colour in her cheeks and a sparkle in her eye that he'd not seen in a long time, and which he was only now beginning to remember.

"How long? How long have you been making art without my knowing? Months? Years?"

His rage converged with a deep sadness. Perhaps this was his fault?—and yet the betrayal that turned through him!

"Just… it's been going on a while."

"And you chose to show him? Someone you've known five fucking minutes?—*my* friend?!—and not me? Your partner that you've lived with for two years, that knows you and wants the best for..."

"But you didn't want the best for me, did you? You just wanted me to fit into the little world you'd planned out for yourself, you only needed me to help you feel better about yourself! I never showed you my work because I knew you'd never truly support it, that you'd never understand."

The kettle began to screech as steam blew from its cap. Malcolm picked it up off the stove and began to pour the water into a pot, trying to remain invisible.

"I can't believe what I'm hearing. You know... you... you're so ungrateful..." George raged.

"For what? Being made to feel like I had to continue with a job that was eating me alive from inside? Being made to feel like I was worthy of nothing else but a clerk for an agency cashing in on every hopeless dreamer in LA?!"

"You wanted... you *needed* a job! And I found one for you because you're too lazy to have found one yourself!"

"I wanted it at the beginning, maybe. I didn't know I'd be made to feel trapped in it when things didn't work out."

"You think I like doing what I do? Working my ass off photographing houses I can't afford, schmoozing with corporate fuck ends just so you can mess around with Malcolm behind my back? Putting together art I didn't even know about..."

"I was scared, alright? I was fucking scared." She shrugged.

"Does anyone want tea?" Malcolm asked through the kitchen alcove.

Tears began to fall from Carry's face as she

looked at George, who looked at her in return as he spoke. "No, Malcolm. I think it's best you leave now and stay somewhere else for tonight. I need to settle this with Carry alone."

"But…"

"Just go. Please. You've done enough damage for one day."

George leant over to Carry and put his arms around her. Open frames and sketches lay scattered on the floor. Malcolm picked up his bag, walked down the stairs and closed the door behind him.

When Carry woke up, the alarm that was dutifully set the night before told her that today was the day of her art show. She slapped her fingers on the desk and searched for her phone. She pressed snooze and closed her eyes. So much had happened.

The empty bed. Cold sheets beneath her on the other side.

She looked at her phone. An image from another time. Must have been two years ago now— of her and George, smiling, glaring into the lens in woolly hats. Looking dumb; looking happy.

She groped downstairs in her dressing gown and switched on the television. The news cast spouting a constant stream of warm anxiety in high, strained voices somehow comforting her. She picked up a magazine. A picture of Brad and Angelina on the front. Something about the break up. She threw it on the sofa, walked over to the kitchen and put in a slice of toast. She looked over to the art pieces on the floor, some of which she still had to frame for tonight.

Tonight. Shit, she thought. What if Malcolm is there? What if he says something to George? What if he says something to her? She told herself to shut up and took a slab of butter from the dish on the side, spreading it on the toast, staring into space.

She began to think about George. He wasn't a bad guy. He just wasn't all that good. Despite everything, despite his efforts to make her feel better, and despite all her perceived laziness, there was something, just partially, innately selfish about him. And this tiny, unfortunate feature, which had become more and more prominent now that she knew it was there, made him, in her eyes, difficult to love.

But *he* tried, occasionally. Didn't he? Yes, he did. Sort of. And because of this *sort of*, she started to wonder if she was the mean one; if she was the brat. She poured cold water into the nozzle of the kettle, and clicked the gas on the stove. Maybe they had just grown apart, and so he *seemed* mean, but actually wasn't. Maybe she was the mean one, for thinking of him as lesser, for fantasizing about Malcolm. Malcolm, who *he*—her partner of over two years—had invited to the house. Maybe she didn't even like Malcolm. Maybe she was creating a mystery around him, around an idiot, just to get at George. Just to provoke another side of him into being, to see what was there, beneath all the crap he'd adopted lately, or to simply get back at him, redeem the tide of resentment that had banked up inside of her, like a locked slog of garbage caught between a dam in a river. If that was the case, she really was mean, wasn't she? But then, she *wasn't* sure this was the case. She was confused, lost and terribly bored of her ongoing condition. She needed something, anything. A bolt of lightning through a window. A sudden shift in the constellations. A deep voice out of the sky, just like in the movies.

She poured herself a cup of rooibos tea and

looked at the mess on the floor. She would do it. She would knock them out at this art show tonight. She heard the news blaze through the room: "...*a hurricane sweeps across Puerto Rico...*" She stared intently at the dense, bitter sketches of disproportioned bodies. She drank a long gulp of hot tea and squeezed her nose. Tonight was the night. Her night. A night when everything would change for the better, and she would become the person she was meant to be all along.

She had remained anxious about the whole thing, wondering whether it was right, whether or not to frantically dial into her phone and cancel. She drove up to the event with George, only the smooth electric sound of their shared Tesla to fill the silence. It was raining lightly across the freeway, black interpolated with streaks of wavy light. George kept asking her if she was okay.

"You're awfully quiet." And then, "I'm proud of you—you know that, right?"

The rain streamed across her passenger window in little giblets. They always made the landscape look an unappealing, soggy beige. Though she was amazed by their jittery strains. Some of the dots, the streaks of rain, moved from a nervous stasis to another place entirely in no time at all. It was like some parts of the universe operated under entirely different laws of physics to her, who could only ever move at a slow, uncertain pace. She remembered the fly she had failed to squat. Waterfalls. Birds. Insects that casually, thoughtlessly climbed vertical columns. She remembered the conversations about quantum mechanics she used to have with George when they'd first met. When they used to smoke weed together out on the rooftop, the sun a filtered, burnt out orange.

Warm and giddy on her skin. She remembered the early, flirtatious period of their relationship, how it had offered them both a refuge from banality which now seemed impossible to reclaim. "I'm proud of you for doing this," he kept repeating in the car, looking over at her anxiously, almost threateningly as he said it, the burning anger beneath it. So that, "I'm *proud* of you," delivered as: *what the fuck happened to us?*

But it was true: what *had* happened to them? She didn't know. She felt that she didn't know anything about herself anymore. All she recognized were the small, micro moments; the movements of her body, her mouth, almost speaking for her, a distinct separation from everything, except a brittle kind of tension; nerves mingled with boredom. In fact, now that the car rolled up into one of the parking spaces outside the café, and she felt a pinch of hesitancy crawl up one side of her face at the thought of actually walking into that damn place and smiling at cruel strangers, she started to question whether this *was* what she wanted at all. Malcolm, when she thought about it, had been rather pushy. A little too eager for someone that didn't even really know her. What was he getting out of this? Was it a game? There was a reason beyond modesty that she didn't want her art to be shown. Perhaps she wasn't ready, and maybe he should have respected that. Her distrust of him began to flare; her face reddened. She blinked, and took in a deep breath.

But then, maybe the gesture was nice. And as she let her mind tail off into dreams of fame and fortune, she wondered if deep down she'd never shown anyone out of conceit. If nobody saw her work, she could always and forever hold on to the idea that she was a mortal, unknown genius. The dream would always be hers.

When she got inside, finally, it wasn't as scary as she'd imagined driving to the event. There was nobody there, which was a relief to Carry, in a way.

The café owner dried his hands on a towel and walked over to her. He put out his hand and she shook it. Her palms were soggy with nerves.

"It's looking great—I'm always amazed how fresh work brings a whole new vibe to the café."

"Yeah, thanks. It's a cool place." She became acutely aware of the sound of her own voice and hated it.

She looked around at the empty white chairs. Her work on the wall was pleasing though. It *did* look good. The frames made them seem less unfinished.

Things gradually picked up and the room began to fill with curious strangers, some of them were actually nice looking, which pleased her. Women with curly hair and guys in sandals with babies attached to their torsos.

She saw Malcolm walk in; George, at the café-bar, engaged in conversation about his photography hadn't noticed him.

He wore a grey beanie which didn't suit the shape of his head, and a brown duffle coat, and he walked straight up to her. He said, "hi," and stared at her, like a lost boy. Not a cute one, she thought; a brat. And not really a boy, she decided. In fact, he looked disheveled; older than the last time she'd seen him; worn-through, like he'd lost his innocence. This sudden clarity, made her question how she'd chosen to see things, how all of us choose to see things, at any stage in our lives. Jesus, he looks old as fuck, she thought to herself. There were lines on his face she'd not noticed before, a kind of arrogance or ignorance.

Maybe it was the bright light. Had she ever really even looked at him? He looked like he'd been living with a pack of wolves for the last week, which she almost said to him, but chose not to. He stood in front of her, arms by his sides.

"I want you to leave with me for New York, tonight. I'm in love with you."

In her dreams, the sentiment would have sounded appealing, romantic. But it came out clunky and lazy, dumb sounding.

She held the smile she'd adopted upon walking into the gallery. The one she'd been practicing. A polite, almost apologetic smile. Then let it go.

"You know you're an idiot, right? I mean, you're aware? Yes?" She said.

"What?" Malcolm's eyebrows furrowed, his eyes seemed to pale.

"What's the matter? Can't take a joke anymore?" She saw George make his clumsy way toward them, and she put her smile back on.

George stopped in front of the now odd seeming pair.

"Malcolm," George nodded, with an air of chivalry. "So, honey, I'm gonna catch a drink with the others, you coming?"

She looked at Malcolm shuffling, his stupid raised eyebrow. Then at George's sad, long face, waiting for an answer, feeling his palpable, wet breath falling on her face. She looked at the pretentious gallery owner, twirling a glass of champagne in his hand, seeming to swivel on his toes as he spoke to a group of giddy girls, and she saw how he wasn't really talking to them, but really just talking to himself.

"Take this," she passed her glass of champagne off into George's hand. She took her coat and pushed the door of the gallery open, walking down the street through the light rain and the crowds, over the crossing and onto the trail, and through the dark woods, hearing the soft flecks of rain on the pine leaves and the muddy ground. She paused at the small lake and lay prostrate across the damp gravel, plunging her hands into the water, filling slowly to the rhythm of rain and tears.

Kenneth Margolin

Proof of Character

Raymond sat on the love seat, and swung his tennis racquet back and forth.

"It's a mental game," he said.

Susan feigned rapt attention. He was regaling her again on the intricacies of tennis. At sixty-five years old, Raymond was thirty years her senior. He recently retired as an attorney—hard driven and successful, she learned when she checked him out before she slept with him. After several miserable relationships with men her own age, Susan enjoyed the company of a man who had lived through his youthful tribulations, and earned some emotional wisdom. *He's good-looking too*, she thought, full head of salt and pepper hair, a ready smile accompanied by crinkle lines around his eyes, medium height, trim. And, he still had muscles. Raymond worked hard at staying fit.

"There are players you will always beat," he said, "and players who will trounce you every time. Let's face it. I couldn't beat Federer on my best day in a thousand lifetimes. You must win against players around your level. The key is character. If you have a strong character, you will prevail—a weak character, you won't."

Susan laughed until she realized that Raymond

was serious.

"That's insane," she said. "You raised two fine children with your wife, even if your marriage wasn't forever. You practiced law for forty years and earned a great reputation. You're telling me that the measure of your character is how much success you achieve in a game you picked up for kicks five years ago?"

"It's not my overall achievement," he said, with a tone of impatience Susan had not heard in their four months dating.

"What matters is my success against players close to my skill level. Take this afternoon. I'll be playing Victor Cheng at the club. He's a small Chinese man who has been playing tennis for decades. He will only play one set at a time, not a whole match. He's slow, his serve is a half-measure above pitty-patty, he chips and lofts and puffs his shots with no pace. He is no fun. I've lost all ten sets I've played against Victor, and I'm a much better player, no comparison."

Susan paused, weighed her words carefully.

"I don't know much about tennis," she said. "If Victor keeps beating you, doesn't that mean he's a better player?"

Raymond stood up. He held his racquet with both hands, and leveled it toward Susan. He flashed the smile that still attracted her.

"No," he said. "I've got Victor's game figured out, and this afternoon, he's mine. Come with me to the club. You've never seen me play."

"We've got a romantic evening planned," Susan said. "I don't want to add pressure on you."

Raymond pumped his fists. "This afternoon," he said, "I welcome pressure. I embrace it. Pressure will be my ally. I won't take no for an answer."

***

Susan sat in the viewing seats above the four indoor courts at Raymond's tennis club. The space was well lit and clean, and the viewing seats comfortable. She settled down with her book until Raymond and the Asian man she assumed was Victor, walked out together to court number two. The other courts were empty. She could hear every sound from below. Susan never understood the lure of ball sports, how a tennis ball, football, soccer ball, baseball, could so engage a player's physical and mental energies. Last week, she watched Raymond in his living room, hold a tennis ball in his hand. He had stared at it, as if there must be within it, some profound wisdom, salvation, if only he could find it.

After Raymond and Victor casually hit the ball back and forth for five minutes to warm up, they met on the opposite sides of the net.

"You serve first?" Victor asked.

"Sure," Raymond said.

The two men walked back to the baselines on their sides of the court. Raymond turned sideways to the court and bounced the tennis ball three times with his left hand. He tossed the ball in the air, and began his service motion. At the moment the ball began to descend from its apex, Raymond hit the tennis ball and sent it whistling into the far edge of the deuce-side service box.

"Wow," Susan said.

Victor barely moved as the ball caromed past his right side—his racquet never touched it.

"Ace," Victor called out. He clapped his racquet face with his left hand.

Raymond served again, and hit another blazing shot, this time to the far edge of the other service box, the "ad-side." Victor's racquet did not come within two feet of the ball as it sailed past him. As Raymond prepared to serve for the third time, Victor moved six inches further behind the baseline, to gain more time to return Raymond's serve. The third serve was as hard as the first two. Victor hit the ball with his racquet frame, and sent it into the net. For the fourth serve, he moved a few inches inside the service line. The moment Raymond's serve hit the ground, Victor met the ball squarely with his racquet, and used the ball's pace to send it looping back over the net. Raymond blasted the return deep to the far right corner, beyond Victor's reach, and the first game was quickly over.

Susan decided to concentrate on the play now, to see if she could glean differences in the two players, besides the obvious chasm between their hitting power. Victor approached the service line and raised his left arm high four times without releasing the ball, his pre-serve ritual. The fifth time, Victor released the ball barely two feet above his head. He pushed the racquet head forward with little speed, and hit the ball, which lazily found the middle of Raymond's service box. Raymond stepped to the left, and hit a streaking forehand winner just inside Victor's right-hand sideline. Three more times, Victor served weakly to Raymond, who smashed the ball to one side or the other, and deprived Victor of a return. Raymond had won the second game without allowing a single rally. Susan could not fathom how Victor ever won a game over Raymond, let alone ten sets.

By the third game, Victor seemed more comfortable with the speed of Raymond's serve and the power of his shots. He returned each serve, with little pace, close to the baseline on Raymond's side of the court. Several extended rallies followed.

Raymond never varied the speed of his shots. He hit them all with fury. Raymond was faster on the court than many young players, and reached Victor's shots easily whereever on the court they landed. Victor's feet were always in motion, ready to move in the direction of Raymond's shot. His problem was that he was simply slow. Raymond hit shot after gorgeous shot close to the lines, and allowed Victor only two points, as Raymond went up three games to none.

Victor used a slice serve to begin game four. As Raymond prepared to strike it back, it skittered wide past Raymond's outstretched racquet. Victor sliced two more serves that caught Raymond off-balance. Raymond shanked them both off the side of his racquet, and into the net. Down forty-love, Raymond finally anticipated the spin of Victor's slice serve, and hit five crisp winners in a row. Raymond turned toward Susan and winked, now up four games to none.

Victor won game five when Raymond tried to end rallies too aggressively, and hit several forehands wide and long. Raymond looked at Susan again, and gave a thumbs up. "No worries," he mouthed. Raymond dialed his strokes back a bit, and won the next six points in a row. Susan had lost track of the score. When she looked at the flip cards attached to the end of the net, that Raymond and Victor used to avoid disputes over the score, she realized that Raymond led five games to one, and was ahead thirty-love in the seventh game, two points away from at last defeating Victor.

Raymond stood at the service line, and bounced on his toes like a boxer just before the bell. He shook his arms to loosen them, and hit a blistering serve into the center of the service box. Victor took a half-step to his left, and blocked it back to Raymond's backhand. Raymond stepped around the ball and aimed an inside out forehand to the far right corner, that missed by three inches. Thirty-fifteen. Raymond seemed determined to end the set with a flourish. He hit the next four serves with no restraint, his second serves as hard as the first. All missed the mark. Raymond was now down thirty-forty. Victor returned Raymond's next serve, and the two engaged in a long rally, Raymond's shots hard and flat, returned by Victor, soft and slow, with compact swings that relied on the pace provided by Raymond's power, not his own. Tennis jiu jitsu. As the extended rally continued, Victor returned an especially vicious forehand, by looping the ball slow and high, just shy of the court's bubble ceiling, and deep. A moonball. Raymond had explained moonballs to Susan, his tone sonorous and intense.

"Real tennis players hate moonballs," he had said. "The rules should outlaw them."

When the moonball finally landed in the far corner of the court to Raymond's backhand, the ball bounced above his shoulder, and forced him to back up as he gauged how to return the shot. He tried a backhand slice that hit the bottom of the net on Raymond's side. Victor had won his second game.

Victor turned the next two games into a moonball fest. Other than his serve, Victor used no other shot. After Victor had hit ten moonballs in a row, Raymond stomped his foot like Rumpelstiltskin.

"Come on, Victor, stop it."

Victor hit another moonball. With each moonball, Raymond tried to hit with more and more power. He sprayed his shots wide, long, and into the net. By the time Victor ended his moonball attack,

Raymond's lead had shrunk to one game, five to four.

Susan understood the importance of momentum in sports. If Victor tied the set at five games apiece, momentum would be his. Victor served softly to Raymond's forehand. As Raymond struck his return, he grunted—"uf"—as he drilled the ball down the line. Victor now anticipated Raymond's predictable pattern of shots, and was quick to the ball. He used his full arsenal of slow-paced shots, more moonballs, and a nasty little slice that caused the ball to bounce low and erratically on Raymond's side of the court. Raymond grunted louder with every shot, and talked to himself during the long rallies.

With sheer power, Raymond won the first two points. His lead was short-lived. Victor went ahead forty-thirty with three perfect drop shots that caught Raymond behind the baseline, unable even with his speed to reach the balls. Raymond hadn't adjusted. He shook his head side to side, then up and down, holding an unfathomable, silent conversation with his inner demons. On the next point, Victor made a mistake. He hit a soft shot to mid-court, exactly in Raymond's forehand wheelhouse. Raymond had an easy put-away. Victor, for once, stood still, resigned to losing the point, which would tie the game at deuce. Raymond pivoted sideways to the ball, and brought his racquet back with perfect forehand technique.

"Faaaaaaaaaak," he screamed, and bludgeoned the ball in the air, past Victor, until it pounded against the backdrop. Raymond wore a self-satisfied expression, looked up toward Susan, and strutted like a peacock displaying for a mate. The set was tied at five all.

If inevitability has not only a sense, but a vibe, the vibe of inevitability thrummed deeply over the courts. Raymond played as if the outcome no longer mattered. He squandered game eleven, as he whaled eight serves in a row, long. He lost the game without scoring a point. Victor served for game twelve. Raymond swatted the first two shots wide, the third long, and the final shot of the set, into the net. Victor had completed his comeback, and won, seven games to five. Raymond approached the net, and with a grimace, shook Victor's hand. Victor spoke to Raymond, in his heavy accent, and without a hint of sarcasm.

"Very good. Maybe next time, you win."

Raymond walked briskly past the locker room and showers, to the parking lot and his car. Susan had not seen him look so distressed. She waited a few minutes to let him settle down, and followed. As she approached Raymond's car, she heard odd noises that she thought may have been a cat in heat.

"Naoooo, naoooo, naoooo."

It was Raymond, who banged his forehead on the steering wheel as he howled. He saw Susan approach, and rolled down his window.

"You need to take a ride share home," he said.

"What." Susan said. "We're having dinner at eight."

"I can't be in a relationship now. Can't you see?"

Susan walked toward the passenger side.

"Drive me home," she said. "We'll talk later."

"We are over," Raymond said.

He rolled up his window, and drove off.

In the weeks following the bizarre breakup, Susan tried to contact Raymond. He would not answer her calls or texts, and blocked her from his social media.

She cried now and then, and enjoyed some self-pity until she acknowledged to herself that it was for the best. Maybe Raymond's meltdown loss to Victor really did reveal some character defect he had kept hidden.

Susan never heard from Raymond again. One Sunday morning, as she drove past a nearby country club, she saw Raymond, head down, muttering to himself, and swinging a golf club back and forth, as he walked toward the golf course.

Rudolfo San Miguel

Return I Will to Old Brazil

When they pulled Ramone Luna off his plane at Los Angeles, he was talking to his wife back in São Paulo after flying overnight from Brazil. His jet was taking on new passengers before continuing to San Francisco. Two men in fine suits waded through the departing travelers and arrested him. They were polite and quiet, escorting him to the airport security center. He was detained in a small white room with a folding chair and a metal table. They took his carry-on bag, everything in his pockets, and his wedding ring. He waited there for several hours. There was no way for him to tell exactly how long. When a short man with thick glasses finally walked into the room, Ramone had been sleeping. They politely woke him up and informed him that he was being arrested for trafficking illegal narcotics. He explained that he was a Samba musician traveling to the San Francisco Bay Area to visit his brother and his family for Christmas. They cordially listened to his explanation then ushered him to a waiting patrol car for transport to a local detention center.

Several days later, in the detention center, Ramone began to worry about whether he would ever see his wife again or be released. He explained several times that he never messed around with drugs except for beer, cigarettes, and occasionally some rum. He asked to see a lawyer and permission to make a call. He was told that his requests were being reviewed. Finally, one day, he was escorted to a small concrete room where he waited for over an hour. The room had a small toilet with a sink and a concrete slab extending from the wall for him to lie down on. There was no light in the room, aside from a small window on the door.

When two men arrived in the room, Ramone was lying face-up on the slab. Both men wore suits. One was considerably bigger than the other. The smaller one was of African descent while the other seemed to come from European lineage; otherwise, he couldn't tell one from the other.

"Getting comfortable?" the smaller man asked, "If we may, we would like to have a short conversation with you, Mr. Luna."

"I apologize," Ramone said, sitting up, "Of course, please let us talk and excuse me again."

"Not at all," the short man said, "My name is Ron Williams, and this is my colleague David Curtis."

"Very pleased to meet both of you."

"I'm afraid we don't have any good news for you, Mr. Luna."

"What is wrong?"

Williams glanced at his partner. "From what we learned, you are an awfully bad man. We have determined that you are more than likely working for Maranhão Cartel as a lieutenant. We are fairly sure that you're using this trip to see your brother as a cover to travel to California for other business. We don't know what that could be."

Upon saying this, Williams walked over and sat next to Ramone.

"Here's the good news," he continued while patting Ramone's shoulder, "If you could provide us information about why you are here and who you're meeting, we can mitigate a transfer to a more comfortable place with supervised access to phone calls."

Williams paused and looked him in the eyes. "What do you think, Mr. Luna?"

Ramone could feel his skin crawl and didn't know what to say. He knew he wanted to get out of that place as soon as possible, go straight home, and never return to the States. "Please, I will help you by any means possible and tell you anything I know. But please understand I am not with any cartel aside from the São Paulo Samba Fellowship."

Williams smirked and looked over at his colleague. His stillness was unnerving to Ramone, who felt sweat dampening his shirt. "I was hoping you wouldn't say that. We need to know why you're here, and we need to figure out the Maranhão Cartel plans. We don't have time. Some of our people are in danger."

"Please, I will help you in any way I can."

"Then tell us the real reason you're here."

"I have…"

"If you fear your employer, you should know we can give you full protection and bring your family here from Brazil."

Ramone tried to remain as calm as possible while he chose the right words. "Mr. Williams, please. I just wanted to see my brother. I don't like to even take medicine from the doctor."

Mr. Williams glanced at his partner again.

Frowning, he got up slowly and stood over Ramone, looking him in the eyes. "Okay, here is where we're at. We have to know what's going on within the next couple of months, and we can't bullshit with you. So, we're going to keep you in this room for an exceptionally long time. We're going to keep you until we decide that you are ready to be honest."

At this point, Ramone was both mortified and angry. He wanted to get up and throw a punch, but he realized the consequences and kept himself in check. "I have! I swear to God, I have. Please!"

"We will be back, maybe in a week or maybe in a month. Until then, you're going to stay here by yourself. You'll be fed, and you'll be kept warm."

At that moment, Williams pointed to the vertical glass slit that acted as the room's window. "See the slit in the door? That is your source of light."

Williams then pointed at a horizontal slot under the window with a small table attached below it. "See that closed slot underneath? That's where meal trays will be dispensed."

"Please," Ramone said, raising his voice further, "What can I do to make you understand that I will help in any ways I can?"

"Oh, that reminds me. David, could you bring in the mattress?"

Williams' companion quickly left the room and returned promptly with a mattress that he propped up against a wall. He pointed at the mattress. "This is your bed. Please don't have an accident on the bed, Mr. Luna. You will not get a replacement. You can use the sink to clean yourself and drink water. You will be given a fresh roll of toilet paper every-other-day with your breakfast."

"Please!"

"Goodbye, Mr. Luna. I hope you think hard about being honest with us the next time we talk."

"But what am I going to do till then?"

"Use your imagination, Mr. Luna. In fact, I'm feeling generous."

Williams riffled through his pocket and pulled out a pack of playing cards, throwing it at Ramones' feet. "Here's a pack of cards I bought at the airport. Take it to kill time while thinking. And think hard about being more honest next time we speak."

Ramone ignored the pack of cards and left them on the floor where Williams dropped them. He was in shock and felt satisfied lying on his mattress, meditating on scenarios in which his probable release would be realized. Between moments of contemplation, he slept.

Days blended together until he lost track of time. He moved only to eat and shit; otherwise, he lay docile, lost in his ideas and dreams. Finally, an hour after awakening from a nightmare, he picked up the pack of cards and dealt a game of Klondike.

He could barely see with what light entered his room. Regardless, he began to play. He lost. He dealt another round, and he won. He dispensed another and gave up halfway through the game. This continued off and on for several more days, at least as far as he could tell, having lost the awareness to comprehend the passage of time.

Eventually, Ramone began to feel the effects of solitude and started talking to himself. These informal conversations mirrored his thoughts. There were also times when he would awaken from vivid dreams and continue discussions that he began in his sleep.

He became restless, lying around and playing

cards with himself. He started exercising randomly throughout his hours, which eventually evolved into a regular routine before meals. He slept less and thought more. His conversations with himself became more complex as his ability to sleep vanished. Soon, he couldn't tell when he slept and when he was daydreaming. He hadn't seen or heard from anyone for what appeared to him a long time—maybe days, maybe months. He couldn't make sense of time anymore. At some point, he decided to change things around.

He'd been playing the only solitaire games he knew—Klondike and Pyramid—and it had become stale. The cards were worn now. He had memorized and studied the pack design, which was all red on the back with a cheap illustration that featured an airline jet lifting off. He examined the font on the playing side—a basic serif—and the artwork on their fronts—detailed but typical. He was bored. He needed something different when he couldn't stand lying on the mattress or running through his exercises.

He decided to play a simple hand of poker with his brother Miguel. This was challenging since Miguel wasn't there nor a gambler. But Ramone was confident that the game would work since Miguel understood the basics of poker. He realized this was crazy. But in light of his situation, he felt he needed to do something before things got worse—before he got worse. Besides, there was no one around to notice his insane behavior.

He dealt two hands of five-card draw. Miguel sat across him in Ramone's mind's eye. Miguel was wearing a bright yellow t-shirt, green khaki shorts, and those aviator sunglasses he liked so fucking much. Smiling like an idiot, he was sure to win the first hand. He was right and took his phantom winnings with a cock-sure grin.

"Good game," Miguel said while smiling, "Let's go again."

"You got it, bro," Ramone replied, returning the smile, "You got it."

He dealt the next hand and was able to win again. Miguel smirked but wanted to continue playing. This went on for roughly three more hands until Miguel was down to his last chips. No one was frowning now. He went all in, swearing under his breath. Ramone saw him lay a pair in front of him. Miguel had three of a kind and took the pot for the first time.

Ramone dealt again, and once again, Miguel went all in. Ramone took the bait. Miguel took everything a second time. Ramone was trying not to frown but went all-in on the first bet. Miguel saw him and showed him a pair of eights. Ramone had nothing.

"Sucker."

"Son of a bitch," Ramone muttered, putting his cards down, "I hate when you pull that kind of shit. When did you learn to play?"

"You're too gullible, brother," Miguel replied, taking the imaginary chips, "I play Texas Hold 'Em Up at Artichoke Joe's with Gina all the time."

At this point, Ramone became tired of playing make-believe, deciding he had a masochistic streak. There was no way Miguel and Gina went to Artichoke Joe's. He had to drag them in there the last time he was in town just to look around. Putting the cards away and laying back on his mattress, he wondered if he would see either of them again. He asked where Dalinda, his wife was now. Was she worried? Has she called the Brazilian consulate yet? If she has, what was the consulate doing? He thought about his mom and

Dad back in Mexico City. What would they think?

His Dad was irritated that he immigrated to Brazil so he could play Samba professionally. Ramone was entranced by Samba, which his father found pathetic. There was something with the way the guitar mixed with rhythms and accented the lyrics and melody. It was like a dream seeping into real life through rhythmic playing, a festival of color and energy. When he was a kid, he would listen to Samba CDs and envision casinos and clubs with exciting women. He'd see fights breakout and escapades untangle during the length of recordings. He'd imagine canvases and houses on cliffs and beaches—young and old intermingling their secrets, crimes, and lusts. He never forgot about those visions. When he grew older, he put his hands on a guitar and another on a plane ticket, leaving his hometown for the streets of São Paulo. That's what he had going for him while lying on the thin foam mattress in his narrow concrete prison— his wife, his guitar, his Samba.

Ramone became restless. His exercise routines throughout the day were beginning to get dull. He was more aware of his narrow cold world. There were times he thought he would scream at the top of his lungs as hard as he could until his throat was raw. Other times, he would cry long and hard. Nothing ever happened. No one ever came. No one cared.

His food was delivered regularly, and every other day he was given a roll of toilet paper. He tried for a while to attract the attention of the person who pushed his tray through his slot, but it was like there was a robot on the other end. He pleaded and complained, but nothing happened. He cried and threw his tray back against the door, but nothing happened. He carried on one-sided conversations with the door, but nothing happened. He prayed to the food guy, begging for mercy, but nothing happened. His food was delivered regularly, and every other day he was given a roll of toilet paper.

Eventually, he passed beyond that phase in his misery, discovering true despair. It was then that he remained in his bed indefinitely, except to relieve himself—he hadn't forgotten what that son of bitch Williams had said about his mattress. He didn't take his trays anymore, nor did he exercise. Ramone laid their defeated and empty, barely having the energy to use the toilet. He lost weight and became weaker every time he awoke. Eventually, he stopped sleeping but remained in this half-awake state of being, a kind of self-hypnosis, which made time passed rapidly. He didn't know how fast but noticed his whiskers exponentially grew as he laid still. He completely lost track of days and truly didn't know if weeks or months had passed.

At some point, Ramone decided to eat. They just delivered his meal, and it smelled really good. In fact, it tasted wonderful—even though it was the same kind of stuff they had been providing him. After finishing, he saw the pack of cards lying on the floor where he left them; it felt like an eon since he played with the cards. He decided to play a couple of more rounds with his brother.

He sat down on the cold floor and began dealing two hands of Texas Hold 'Em, just to entice Miguel. He looked up, and there, his brother was sitting on the floor across from him. This time though, it was more than Ramone's imagination constructing a ghost in the nothingness. Miguel was there. And Ramone didn't question his presence.

Miguel was wearing the same clothes he wore the other times. He was stretching out like they were about to play some tennis instead of cards. Ramone shook his head and thought about how much his brother loved to ham it up around him.

"You ready to go, buddy?"

"Let's do this."

Ramone stretches out to get himself ready and realized that they were no longer in a concrete cell. They were sitting in the sand right outside Clube do Paraíso, where he had regular gigs. It was near sunset. There were a handful of people at the bar and a solo player performing. Ramone figured it was the middle of the week. It was then that he felt something was wrong.

"Miguel, for some reason, I don't think we're supposed to be here."

Miguel took his cards. "The club doesn't own the beach or the sand, brother. No one's going to bust us."

"Oh, okay. That has reason."

They played a couple of hands. This time Ramone was aware of Miguel's skills, and things were a little more even.

"Shouldn't you be in San Bruno with Gina? I mean, are you both here, or is it just you?"

"We're here on vacation," Miguel said, lying down in the sand, "Remember?"

"My apologies. My head has been in other places lately. I think I got a concussion or something."

"What do you mean? I'm getting a concussion listening to you."

"No, it's just I swear I was in jail before we started playing."

Miguel sat up and looked at Ramone. "In jail?

This doesn't look like a jail. Were you in jail recently or something like that?"

"I thought so. I don't know. Fuck it, right? Where's Gina?"

"With Dalinda. Let's get a drink and catch a cab home."

They walked over to the bar and ordered some beers as the sunset receded into the twilight. The beach was warm, and the lights of homes in Guaruja's beach community were visible. Ramone sipped his beer and looked towards the ocean. It was then he realized that none of this experience was really happening. He was still in his narrow concrete room. He was staring at his cell door. Beyond that was the mysterious landscape of the detention center. Beyond that was the world at large. Beyond that were Dalinda and Brazil. It was there that that beach was located in the coastal town of Guarujá near São Paulo. But Ramone was still in his narrow concrete room.

He lay on his mattress for a couple of hours, trying to process what happened. He had been in his cell for a long time, but then he hadn't. He had been on the beach in Brazil with his brother. It was real, but so was his life in the concrete room. Ramone wondered what life was and what was fiction, then considered whether it mattered.

He looked back at his door and noticed they had served him another meal. It seemed like he just ate, but he also felt burning bangs of hunger as if he hadn't eaten for days. Getting up, Ramone took his tray, devouring its contents. He drank some water from his sink, used the toilet, and cleaned up. Soon after, he exercised again for the first time in a while, feeling rejuvenated and spry.

***

The problem was what to do with his energy. After playing a couple of more hands of Klondike, Ramone thought about how long he had been in the concrete room. It must have been months since he was imprisoned, but then he decided it couldn't have been that long—maybe only several weeks. He couldn't tell but felt that his jailors would return soon. He focused his thoughts on that. Specifically, what he should do when they returned.

He quickly decided he was going to have to lie. They didn't want to hear the truth; they wanted him to tell them they were right. The problem was how he was going to play them. He thought about this a lot while playing solitaire until he grew tired and went back to his mattress. He lay down and tried to rest, but he was too restless. He sat up on the side of the bed and looked at the opposite wall, then closed his eyes and prayed.

"Hey Ramone," a voice said in the quiet of the concrete room, "You aren't sleeping, are you?"

Ramone sat up, opening his eyes—looking in the direction of the voice. There was nothing but his toilet and sink. He looked to the cell door, which was the same as always. He clamored toward it and looked through the window slit. Nothing was there but the wall adjacent to his cell door. The voice seemed to come from his room, though. He went and sat back down on his mattress.

His nerves were fried. It seemed like his hosts were messing with him now. He closed his eyes and prayed some more.

"Hey Ramone," the voice said again, "Wake the fuckup; we're almost there!"

Ramone slowly opened his eyes and looked around his empty concrete room. He considered whether he was talking to himself and not aware of it before dismissing the notion as crazy. It was then that something happened that he truly never expected to ever occur in his life, though consciously he was expecting and hoping for it to happen. His cell door opened.

He blinked his eyes several times from the glare of light in the hallway. The brightness was overwhelming, and he could barely see the silhouette of the two men outside the entrance. The larger of the two men walked into the room. Ramone noticed his uniform and recognize him as one of the detention guards.

The guard kept his game face on and looked at him as if beckoning him to make a move. Ramone looked into his eyes, which were as cold as the concrete in the cell.

Soon after, the other man walked in. He was about Ramone's height and wore a maroon medical scrub. He had a serious expression on his face but more in-line with someone focusing their attention on a task at hand. He looked at the guard briefly.

"Mr. Luna," the guard barked, "Thank you for your continued patience. Please allow Dr. Brand to perform a momentary examination to determine your ongoing health. This is mandatory, and any unexpected behavior deemed hostile will be dealt with in a swift and meaningful manner. Do you understand what I have said, sir?"

Ramone wondered if this was another fiction his mind had created. He didn't know what to say and was far from making a movement or any bullshit like that.

"I repeat. Do you understand what I have said, sir?"

"Yes."

The medic then went about performing a complete physical on Ramone while he sat there completely still. Ramone had no energy to move and was in shock by the sudden appearance of other human beings. Also, he contemplated the veracity of their existence in his concrete landscape.

After the medic was finished, he asked him some questions, which Ramone answered briefly as the medic made notes. Most of the queries were simple. How was he sleeping, and was he experiencing anything unusual? This question made Ramone laugh to himself. He also asked questions like his name, including basic information about himself and where he was now. The guard stood behind the medic, stone-faced and glaring. When the medic was finished with his questions, he looked at the guard then walked out of the room.

The guard began backing out of the room. "Thank you for your cooperation and continued patience. Have a nice day."

"How much longer till I can leave? I mean, how long until I will have a follow-up conversation about my case?

The guard closed the door. "Have a nice day."

Ramone was again alone in his concrete room. The silence was unbearable. He lay back down and thought about what he should do next. He considered over-analyzing what just happened but couldn't get his mind to focus on anything aside from the silence. It beckoned him into a meditative state of emptiness, both in thoughts and feelings. He found it refreshing and began to feel a vibration around him. Thinking it was because of the shock he had a moment earlier, he began to recognize the shaking as a sensation he felt while driving.

He opened his eyes and confirmed what he felt. It was warm and humid. He was sitting in an SUV on the main road back to São Paulo. His brother was driving casually. There was some kind of Mexican Hip-Hop on the stereo. The stench of Miguel's cigars was everywhere inside the truck.

"Fuck man," his brother said, glancing at him, "You were sleeping like a rock, Ramone. When's the last night you slept, buddy?"

Ramone was confused but slightly relieved. He sat up straight and tried to clear his head. "I had some crazy dreams."

"No shit?"

"No," Ramone replied, glancing at his brother, "Just like this situation where I get locked up in the states when I was trying to visit you and Gina."

"What? Did they catch you with drugs and shit?"

"No, but they thought I was a big shot with some cartel."

"Huh. Well, that sucks. Did you even get some dream time partying it up when they got you?"

"No"

"Well, that really sucks."

"Hey, where are we going again?"

"So, like, don't tell anyone I said anything, but we're heading to this bar to have a drink."

"Oh, what does that mean?"

"It's a surprise party, dumb-ass. Dalinda rented out the whole place, but it is supposed to be like I'm taking you there for some drinks for your birthday, just you and me."

"Oh, it's my birthday?"

"Oh man, you better go back to sleep, buddy."

Ramone felt someone nudging his shoulder and looked over at his brother. But he wasn't there. He looked in front of him and found himself staring at the wall of his concrete room. He was nudged again, and this time notice Ron Williams standing beside him while he sat on his bed. Williams had a concerned looked on his face and silently examined him for a moment.

"Mr. Williams? Are you real?"

Williams was alone this time. His partner wasn't there, nor was there a guard. The concrete room's door was open behind him. Williams scratched his chin before saying anything. "Mr. Luna, do you realize you were talking to yourself just now?"

"No, I was asleep."

"With your eyes open?"

"I guess."

"Well, Mr. Luna," Williams said, sitting beside him, "You've been doing that for quite a while, and, in some cases, you've been shouting out loud. My associates are beginning to get concerned."

"Oh, are we going to have another conversation? Because I am ready to tell you everything."

Williams brushes his knee and stretches. "That will not be necessary, Mr. Luna, we have cleared you, and you are no longer considered a person of interest. Frankly, the Brazilian consulate has been lobbying for your release after everything that has happened. We sincerely apologize for such long incarceration. There have been several amnesty organizations that have also been petitioning for your release. I am afraid that we have made an extremely serious error. And I sincerely and deeply apologize for your treatment. We will fully compensate you for any health-related expenses you may have incurred, including mental health treatment. I am also authorized to provide you with an extremely generous financial compensation package with your signature on several liability release forms. We can discuss those items and a couple of others at a later time once you have had a chance to recover."

"May I call my wife?"

"Well, that, unfortunately, is the bad news I have for you. It appears your incarceration has reached the cartels in Brazil. Apparently, a rival cartel took it as an opportunity to take hostages as leverage against the Maranhão Cartel. I am afraid they were able to locate your wife and daughter."

"Are they alright?"

"I am sorry to tell you that both were killed once Maranhão Cartel refused to cooperate with the other cartel. I am so sorry, sir."

Ramone said nothing and continued to stare at the wall.

"So, if you wouldn't mind," Williams said, getting up slowly, "Could you please remain here for a short while longer. I will leave the door open. A medical examiner will be in a few moments for a quick check. He will then escort you to a very nice room with a patio where you will reside for a day or two until we can finalize your release. I am authorized to take you wherever you want. Your passport will be in your room, along with all your possessions. You are more than welcome to continue your journey to San Francisco to visit your brother. We can also transport you to your remaining family in São Paulo. Please let me know if there is anything I can do for you."

"Thank you. I guess."

***

Williams left quietly.

Ramone continued to stare blankly at his wall. He looked for something in the concrete that might reveal that this was just another fiction created by his mind. That he was still trapped in his small home while his family was safe in São Paulo. He couldn't convince himself of anything, though, as the hallway light poured into his room from the open door. He squeezed his eyes tightly together to block the light. He began to pray.

"You know," a voice said, "No matter how much you pray, life will continue unchanged."

"What do you know?" Ramone muttered, opening his eyes and looking at the concrete wall.

"I know that you wanted this moment to happen for so long," the voice answered, "Only to realize how much it has cost you."

"I never was told the price," Ramone said to the wall.

"No one ever is. That is life, as they say. In fiction, things are the way we make them. But in life, this is not always the case."

"This is not very comforting. You're not helping."

"What do you want me to tell you? This is life."

Ramone thought about this for a second. Then he looked around him for the source of the voice. He was alone. He thought maybe if he closed his door, he would see who he was talking to. It would at least make things more comfortable. And so, he got up and closed the door. Returning to his mattress, he waited for the voice to show itself, but nothing happened. Ramone closed his eyes.

"Well," he whispered to the empty room, "If this is life, then give me fiction."

It was then that he heard a woman singing a plaintive note to some Brazilian ballad before the Samba orchestra began performing their rhythmic melody about beach sunsets and the coastal moan of the ocean.

Ramone opened his eyes to see the club Miguel had mentioned. He'd been there before. He recognized most of the people. The band was on a small platform, and the middle-aged woman singing had a broad smile. To his left was Dalinda in her lavender party dress walking towards him. She walked over with a drink, and they kissed. They strolled together to the dance floor, where couples had already begun to dance.

He could hear a voice echo from somewhere far in the distance. It was Williams' voice. He was talking to someone else. There was a concern in his tone. Ramone couldn't make out what was being said and lost interest; instead, he focused on Dalinda and the music.

"What's wrong, baby?" Dalinda whispered in his ear.

Nothing, my love. You look wonderful tonight. Your just as I always remember in my mind's eye."

Ramone smiled, humming along with the samba music. He danced with his wife and bantered with his brother and some friends. The twilight dimmed the sky above. The warm and humid air saturated the packed club. It was such a great evening that he never wanted to leave São Paulo again. Yet William's voice beckoned. So Ramone closed his eyes, held tight to his wife, and sang along with the Samba performers.

Norbert Kovacs

Pool Party

Rick Patterson wanted his five-year-old son Jay to become a high achiever. Rick had been an ambitious type himself when young—if not from five years of age. An A student in grade school, he graduated from a well-admired college, secured a job at a major Hartford insurance company, and advanced to a top manager role. He felt he could guide Jay to a similar outcome as the boy already boasted much to recommend him. Jay had handsome looks, for one, with his pale blonde hair and wonderful, clear blue eyes. He had a strong, tight body that showed energy and promised to become athletic. Several of Rick's friends liked to say the boy looked "the little man."

So Rick went to goading his son to become a success. He took Jay outside to practice at soccer and sought for signs of latent, athletic talent. He ran, passed, and kicked the ball with the child sometimes for an hour, a rather long time for a five-year-old to play. Jay would cry before the end of it and ask that they stop. The father relented with disappointment. But it was only long after their exercise on the lawn that Rick regretted pushing the boy. He is only five after all, he told himself. He is supposed to be having fun.

Rick happened to have some guilty thoughts along these lines the evening his wife Sue told him that Jay had been asked to a birthday party by a boy at his morning preschool.

"Tell Daddy what kind of party it will be," Sue asked Jay who sat beside her at the dinner table.

"It'll be a POOL party! They gonna have a POOL!" The boy yelled the news as if it must impress his father.

Mr. Patterson smiled. "I'm glad to hear it. I bet you'll have a lot of fun there." Then to his wife, he added, "It'll be a good opportunity for him to make some new friends. He should be trying even at his age. That will put him ahead socially in grade school."

"I'm sure he will, dear. But promise to stop by the party on your way home from work Friday. The Cowleys are on Walnut Street, a blue house, number 37. You can see him with the other kids who'll be there. I'm sure Jay would be too happy if you came."

"If I'm not kept late, I will be."

"You know, tomorrow afternoon, I plan to go buy him these neat purple and black swimming trunks for the thing." Sue prided herself on her taste in fashion, even when it came to her child as she shared her husband's ambition for the boy. "I think they'll make him look the greatest kid there."

"Of course, he'll be the sharpest one. He'll be the friendliest, kindest, smartest boy, too. Won't you Jay?"

The parents turned to their son. While they had been preening themselves on the coming party, Jay had piled his spoon high with vegetables and tilted it at a precarious angle. With a sudden spring, he now launched his peas and carrots at the wall opposite the table, where they landed with a huge splat. His parents cried out, but the boy smiled with mouth open wide.

After a full, busy day at work that Friday, the day of the birthday party, Rick decided he would stop by the Cowleys as he had promised. Had the other kids taken to Jay?, Rick wondered as he neared the exit closest the Cowleys' part of Wethersfield. Has he impressed them as an athlete? A friend? He became more eager to know as he imagined each new way the child might excel.

At the Cowleys' front door soon after three, Rick told the red-haired woman who greeted him that his son Jay was at the party and that he had come to see him. "I'm the proud father." To his surprise, the woman glared.

"Haven't you arrived at a good time?" she said. "Your kid has made the Cowleys fuming mad. Mr. and Mrs. Cowley are on the deck setting your wife straight over him—if they aren't still yelling."

"Oh?" Rick entered the house and found mothers soothing and comforting several frightened children around the living room. He stalked past them toward the screen door that led to the outside deck. Angry voices sounded beyond it, his wife's high among them.

The Cowleys had ushered Sue Patterson and Jay into their home with smiles and welcomes at one p.m. that afternoon. They had led the mother and her son to the backyard deck, where, not far below, numerous children played in a two-foot tall wading pool that covered a good patch of the yard. The children were in a great spree of splashing, kicking, and dousing each other with water. Before releasing Jay to them, Sue whispered in his ear, "You look sharp as a pin.

The others will like you for it," and gave him a happy jiggle. Jay moved off with confidence; once in the pool, he called loudly as he joined several kids in play splashing. Soon, he had made a number of new friends.

Sue Patterson settled into a chair on the deck overlooking the pool. The mothers of the other children were scattered around the back of the deck or in the house, chatting importantly about things of small consequence: hair styles, talk shows, Tupperware. Facing Sue in another seat was Carrie Cowley, whose son Ben was having the birthday, his fifth. Carrie Cowley had frizzy, drab hair that appeared untended; her makeup did little for what Sue considered a boring face. The woman's shirt and pants sagged in many places though she was not fat. Can't dress herself, Sue decided. Carrie was elaborating on her home and family, and Sue found she did not care much for it. Besides her part-time secretary role, Carrie seemed to have little like a life but appeared strangely happy despite it. Her husband John, a thin, spare man, was a supervisor at a local factory. "A full-time role," Carrie said, which nearly made Sue snicker. Rick, she believed, did much better in his post at the insurance company. More of Carrie's faults surfaced as they continued. She inquired little when Sue plunged into the details of her own life. She let her eyes droop when Sue described her newly renovated home and the pluses of her husband's job. In all, Sue felt Carrie Cowley a poor match as a conversation partner. It'll be a grin-and-bear-it afternoon, she told herself.

As the mothers spoke, the kids ran screaming and yelling from the pool for the deck to grab the melon and apple wedges that Mr. Cowley had set on the outside table. The children gulped these down, letting the juice dribble down their chins, then chased each other screaming around the deck. The unmindful among them tripped, fell on the deck's hardwood, and wailed piteously. In the midst of the melee, a boy, armed with two fistfuls of dirt and dandelions, ran after a girl sporting a neatly braided ponytail. The girl fled, crashing into people all over the deck. Her cries drove the other children into a howling fury. As the screams reached their height, the children sped back to the pool where they resumed drenching each other. In the children's wake, the mothers surveyed the ruined deck dumbfounded, trying to comprehend. But the women soon dismissed their children's violence. "Spirited play," they called it.

At last, the kids were hailed as a group onto the deck and gathered round the table where Mrs. Cowley installed a large, white birthday cake. After everyone sang "Happy Birthday" to Ben, the mothers cut the cake, and the kids fell on it greedily. Sue watched the event with disgust. She turned away as an obese, little girl consumed her cake in two bites. At the other extreme was Ben Cowley, a thin, pale child who ate almost with reluctance. Probably over-petted, Sue thought. Must get sick easily—and with a mind for his mother to fawn on him. The one child Sue admired eating was her own. Yes, Jay did have two slices of cake when Mrs. Cowley insisted everyone have only one. But Sue told herself Jay was growing and on his way to becoming a strong, physically commanding adult: he needed some extra to get him there. He, at least, was not growing *outward* like the others.

The children finished the cake and ran back to the yard. Half went to the "slip-and-slide" that Mr. Cowley had fetched a distance from the pool and was dousing with water. A few alongside two of the mothers went to a corner of the lawn to play "throw and hit" with a whiffle ball. The remaining children hung out in the pool. Sue had held back Jay to clean his face of any signs of cake.

"You know something," she said softly as she wiped the last of the frosting from his lip. "I think you're turning out the most popular kid at the party. You should feel proud."

When his mother gave him this endorsement, Jay was watching the pool where his new friend Greg talked with Ben Cowley. Since they were acquainted an hour and a half ago, Jay and Greg had splashed and yelled more often, besides scared and frightened more of the other children, than anyone else at the party. Jay felt a bond with Greg over it, in fact believed himself to be Greg's exclusive friend forever (or at least until the party ended). So he was upset to see Ben approach the boy and try to talk with him. Ben's thinness, his care and politeness toward Greg all were contemptible to the Patterson boy, though Jay had been friendly to him earlier. Jay fidgeted in his mother's grasp as he thought to set Ben straight on who was friends with whom. Sue, who only imagined her child was uncomfortable to be wiped so long, let him go and smiled as he bound back to the pool.

Sue returned to her beach chair by the deck's edge as Carrie Cowley took a seat by her again. Carrie was sharing ideas on how parent-mentors might improve Ben and Jay's preschool (and boring Sue with it) when she happened to look up toward the pool. "OH!" she cried. "You let go of Ben this instant, do you hear?"

Sue, who had her back to the yard, turned. She saw Jay at the far side of the pool holding little Ben Cowley's head under water. The boy evidently had been restrained so for several seconds, for his legs floated at odd angles in the pool behind him. Greg watched it happen without interfering as did several other children on the lawn. The punishment Jay inflicted on Ben over Greg had turned into a party-wide spectacle.

"Jay, let go of Ben right now," Sue said beside herself.

With a shove of Ben's head, Jay let go his victim who righted himself and gasped for air. Mr. Cowley rushed to the poolside and drew Ben to his chest. After finding the boy okay, he faced Jay and said, "You need to control yourself!"

"Get out of that pool—now!" Mrs. Cowley yelled at the child from the deck. "And don't you bother Ben anymore."

His head raised proudly, Jay climbed from the pool with Greg and trudged toward the "throw and hit." Their departure drew a close to the violent spectacle. The children around the lawn returned to their games, and Mr. Cowley stalked back to the water slide, giving Jay a last shake of the head.

On the deck, Mrs. Cowley turned an aggrieved face toward Sue, who was ready for it. "I think I'm as shocked as you are, Mrs. Cowley," she said, her mouth open like an O. "I can't imagine how he thought to do it. He won't do anything of the kind again. I promise."

These words sated Mrs. Cowley, who let her frown drop. The two mothers slowly resumed their conversation of earlier. Sue complimented the Cowleys' house and the party food, not with sincerity but to avoid looking any worse to her hostess.

The party had passed its golden hour. Half the mothers took their kids home in the next twenty minutes. The remaining children played sedately in the pool or ambled the lawn. Carrie Cowley chatted with Sue who became newly reluctant to hear it. As things quieted, Mrs. Cowley looked past the deck and yelled for the second time. In the part of the pool closest the two women, Jay again was holding Ben's head under water. How this second dunking came to pass was so: resenting his eviction from the pool where Ben was allowed to stay, Jay had snuck back when no adult was watching. After Greg followed suit, Jay warned Ben through a scowl and an angry splash to let them alone. Feeling hard against them, Ben had drawn to Greg in defiance. Jay went on the offensive then.

Sue turned to find the scene the same as earlier. The fact it could be seemed rather ironic. Hadn't I promised this wouldn't happen?, she thought. Yet there he was dunking Ben as if his warning had gone in one ear and out the other. It struck Sue as funny somehow, despite her recognizing it should not. She suppressed any sign of this as she followed Mrs. Cowley toward the poolside.

Jay released Ben as he saw the two women descend the stairs from the deck. Mrs. Cowley went and drew her son gasping from the water and into her arms. As her husband came, Mrs. Cowley cried to Jay, "How can you do that—and a *second* time? Well?" She glared and turned to Sue for support.

Sue realized she must speak. As can happen when people suddenly have to be serious, Sue did not manage very well: her voice came barking like a dog as she said, "Jason, control yourself!" When she considered how fierce she sounded, her lips curled helplessly and, before she knew it, she smiled. Jay responded quickly: he gave over any thought of being punished and laughed. The sound of it infected his mother and she laughed too.

Mrs. Cowley grew dark. "I don't see what is so funny about your son suffocating my child," she said.

Sue suppressed herself. "I'm sorry," she said and again faced Jay. She studied him a moment as if to learn whether he would erupt a second time. By some ill luck, Jay imagined her look meant that she was amused still; gleeful over it, he cried, "Hurray!" and sent the water around him skyward in a splash. Sue found this too much and laughed.

"Mrs. Patterson," Carrie Cowley said, scowling, "I cannot accept this humor of yours. Please remove your son and yourself from my home this minute."

Sue was sobered and understood she must comply. "I am sorry. We will go. Jay, come." With a glum face, Jay climbed from the pool; Sue got her towel from the deck and dried him. When Sue turned to say goodbye to Mrs. Cowley, Carrie said, "I guess you'll think to act maturely around your child now."

Sue went cold. "And what does that mean?"

"Well, children model off their parents. How will he turn out when you act like assaulting a friend is so funny?"

Sue stared. "I don't think a poorly timed laugh gives you the right to call me a bad parent."

John Cowley stepped forward, glaring. "Why not quit acting so mighty? Your kid attacked *mine*, remember?"

"Isn't that a bit much? Jay didn't exactly kill Ben."

"No, but he tried. He should feel lucky I didn't whack him."

"So, you want to make threats? Well, I won't put up with it..."

"Then go," Mrs. Cowley said, standing a little

straighter. "We asked you to leave."

As the women spoke, Rick Patterson, who newly had arrived, came onto the deck. "Hey now, what's this?" he asked, descending the deck's stairs. "Sue, what on earth happened? What is this I heard about Jay?"

Sue threw back her head indignantly. "What happened is that the Cowleys are throwing Jay and me out from the party; they threatened to be violent with him, too."

"What?" Rick colored.

"That isn't what I said," Mr. Cowley said. "You're misrepresenting things."

"Should you say what's misrepresented after those comments you and your wife made to me?" Sue tried to sound angrier than she was, hoping it would move her husband. It did.

"Here, what exactly did you say?" Rick asked Mr. Cowley.

"When your kid beats mine up, I can say something, can't I?"

"As if five year olds are beating up anybody," Rick said, still ignorant of the case.

"But that is what happened," Mr. Cowley yelled. "He beat up my boy Ben in the pool. Like a *thug*." Cowley barked this last word at Jay, who had hid halfway behind his mother. The man's anger frightened the boy, and he broke into a wide-mouthed sob.

Sue shook her head. "I won't take any more of this." She faced her husband. "These people are stupid and mean-minded. I'm going home this instant." She dragged Jay, still crying, across the lawn toward her car in front of the house.

Mr. Cowley walked a few steps in her direction.

"Don't think your brat will get off so easy if he tries anything again with my kid—not at that preschool or anywhere else!"

Sue disappeared with her son around the corner of the house without turning.

Rick Patterson snarled at Mr. Cowley. "Hey, watch your mouth! You can't yell like that at a mother and her five-year-old."

"Your brat and your wife ruined my kid's party. I think I can say something."

"You have some nerve calling my kid a brat!"

Mr. Cowley glared. "You take back that remark!"

"I'm not." Rick drew up straight, head raised.

The mothers with the last remaining children herded them into the house as the men shot their angry words. The yard was clear when John Cowley and Rick Patterson drew together snarling. One man stepped too close and suddenly they were pushing. Fists swung. The men fought, punching hard, circling the backyard. As they drew toward the trees, Rick knocked into John Cowley and the two fell tussling on the ground. Neither had a thought to surrender.

The two were wrestling still when they heard singing from the street. The men stopped as they saw a girl, perhaps five years old, riding past the lawn on a pink bicycle decked with red ribbons. She sang a child's happy song as she swung her head side to side. She did not notice the men on the lawn. When the girl had passed, Rick and John faced each other self-consciously.

"Here," John started slowly, "why are we fighting like a pair of animals? What is this proving?"

"Yeah, I'm wondering too." Rick studied the grass shyly.

"How about washing up inside?"

Rick wiped a trickle of blood from his mouth. "No, I'm fine. I think I'll go, however."

"Are you sure? It won't be a problem?"

"I'm positive. I don't need to scare those mothers and their kids any more than I have."

"Well... Have a pleasant drive home."

"Enjoy the rest of your day."

Rick Patterson stumbled toward his car in front of the house. He stopped once on the lawn to survey his clothes. He saw they were torn and sweat soaked. Blood spotted his shirt front. I'm a mess, ain't I?, he thought. He reached his car and found the windows blinding bright in the summer sun.

Rick nursed an ice pack against his head as he sat on his living room couch. Sue sat beside him offering her sympathy. "I never thought it would come to a fight," she said, stroking her husband's shoulder.

"Really?" Rick said with some doubt. "Everyone sounded like they would claw each other dead when I got there."

"Still, it ended worse than it should have. Do you think you'll be okay?"

"I'll be fine. I'm worried more about how you behaved."

"What about it?"

"They had a point about Jay not abusing their kid. He won't get ahead hurting people. You shouldn't have defended him."

"You may be right." Sue looked at the ground, avoiding his eye, as she pressed down her lip.

Rick took the ice pack from his head and laid it on the couch. "This ice isn't helping like I thought. Where's Jay? I haven't seen him since I got home."

"He's out back playing."

Rick went to the window and saw Jay kicking a soccer ball against the back yard's stone wall. As he watched, the landline phone rang in the kitchen. The answering machine started and Mrs. Cowley's voice sounded. Rick strode toward the phone. As he neared it, his wife came from the living room and intercepted him.

"Don't pick up the phone!" she warned. "After all that Cowley woman said, I don't want either of us to speak to her."

Rick crinkled his brow. Wasn't that a very hot judgment, he thought, after she had seemed so sorry just now? But he held silent as Mrs. Cowley said on the answerer, "My husband and I would like to talk with you about the party—and some of the things I said." The woman's voice slowed as if she were embarrassed. "Please call us back, our number is—"

Sue smirked with a note of righteousness. "Well, it sounds like Carrie Cowley realizes she stepped out of line. She knew she opened her fat mouth a little too much."

Mrs. Cowley ended her message, setting her phone down with a click. "Let's call them, " Rick said at once. "You're going to apologize to her. You and Jay incited them." He reached for the phone.

"Are you kidding? Apologize? I mean, seriously apologize?"

"Yes. I will too since I baited Cowley into that fight."

"I'm not apologizing to them. I can't."

"No, you will or I'll give *you* a good piece of my mind." He glared at her the same way Mr. Cowley had him on the lawn.

Sue quailed. "Fine. I will. But give me a minute

to think of what to say. I have to figure how to make this delicate."

"Take your time. I'll be outside with Jay whenever you're set."

Rick went onto the house's deck and down the stairs to the lawn where his son Jay was kicking his soccer ball at the stone wall. "Hey guy, can I play too?"

"Sure," the child chirped. Rick came up. As he kicked the ball with the boy, he saw Jay smile. Jay did not seem bothered by any memory of the party nor the scolding that made him sob. He can because he's young, Rick thought. All the better for him: he could have developed a complex. The father and son kicked the soccer ball back and forth gently; Rick's interest now was that they have fun like any two friends. He doesn't need to become an adult before he gets to be a child, the father considered.

Edward Ahern

The Souvenir

It wasn't a bribe, exactly. But it was a smuggle. I'd called ahead to the shop on 47th Street in New York, and the owner showed me a selection of jade pendants. I recalled the woman who would wear it, and examined pieces until I found one that would punctuate her grace and beauty. The oval pendant was green Burmese jade with lotus flowers carved into it. I paid a lot of cash.

A week after buying the pendant I flew with it to Malaysia. On arriving in Kuala Lumpur I carried the pendant through customs in the same pocket as my loose change, declaring nothing. Once installed in the Shangri-La hotel I took a gift box out of my suitcase and set in the pendant. I hadn't worried about the smuggling, customs officials rarely look closely at incoming foreign businessmen.

Before I numbed out from jet lag, I made several calls to reconfirm appointments for the next day.

"Ashraf bin Shukri, please. It's Fred Malone... Ashraf?... It's Fred. Fine, thank you. And you?... And we're still on for dinner as well?...Great, see you at 10:00."

After I hung up, I felt a twinge of guilt. It wasn't Ashraf I was really looking forward to seeing, it was the company he kept. I reconfirmed three more appointments, skipped the raid on the minibar and went to bed.

At ten the next morning I was in his office. Ashraf was Bumiputra, native Malay in a society where the ethnic Chinese men increasingly controlled business and money. But the Malays still controlled the politics and government institutions, and Ashraf was the number two man at the national construction company. To which I sold tens of millions of dollars-worth of equipment.

"You look well, Ashraf."

The lie was polite; he always looked gaunt, and his dry cough seemed worse.

"And you still look a little overstuffed."

We smiled. We both trusted and liked each other.

I set the gift box on his teak desk. "Here's that souvenir from New York that we talked about."

"Thank you." He took the box and, without opening it or mentioning the recipient, gently set it in his middle drawer.

"Our engineers tell me that the equipment is running well. Any problems or issues I should know about?"

"Let me get Li in here so we can discuss specifics."

Li Wen He was Chinese, was the senior finance manager, and was the man who told me with precision where our equipment performance wasn't up to expectations. Ashraf spoke during these sessions only to ask Li to confirm if what I'd said was accurate, and to give his approval to our negotiated settlements.

Li and I would never be friendly enough to hug, but he gave honest appraisals. I thought of him as Cai Shen, the god-accountant who guarded the heavenly treasuries. He didn't beat me up too badly during his review, and I left a little before noon.

After three more appointments. I was feeling pretty granular, and went back to the Shang for a shower, then dressed for dinner. I was hosting at the Lafite restaurant in the hotel, popular with business travelers but not with the locals. Ashraf always requested that we eat there, either because it was his infrequent chance at French cuisine or because he thought I'd feel more comfortable. Or perhaps because he felt it was more discreet. There was no paper trail of his presence.

He arrived Malay promptly, about fifteen minutes late. And brought Meili.

Her western name was Jane, which she used only when she had to with occidentals. The meaning of her Chinese name was beautiful and graceful, which she was. She was wearing the jade pendant.

Every time I met her, I knew why Ashraf, a man with two wives, had desired her as a mistress. Aside from being slenderly attractive, she had the unpurchaseable gifts of taking delight in simple things and welcoming others into her company. But not in a submissive way. Her eyes glittered with intelligence and her comments gently poked at anything pompous or unfeeling.

"Maili, always a treat to see you." We shook hands, hers held out almost as if as if it should be kissed.

"Fred, you are looking prosperous." I smiled. Her comment was a gentler version of Ashraf's.

She wore a shantung silk cheongsam in pale

green that counterpointed the jade, as if she'd seen the jewel before it's arrival and dressed accordingly. Ashraf had changed his office baju melayu-a loose tunic- to an embroidered evening one

"How goes the studio?"

Ashraf was subsidizing Maili in a small studio where she taught Tai Chi and Pilates. I doubted if her students were ever able to approach her grace in motion.

Maili's smile was slightly dour, and her words almost hid the barb about a woman's role still in Malaysia. "It's fulfilling to see women attain new levels."

They carefully perused the menus, squinting at the smaller English translations under the French descriptions, then ordered what they always did. -Ashraf a filet with bearnaise sauce and Maili a sautéed pork and vegetable dish. As we waited to be served Ashraf's phone buzzed twice, which he ignored. On the third angry buzzing he coughed and excused himself, ostensibly to go to the bathroom. I was grateful for the chance to focus on Maili.

Her eyes opened slightly more. "Thank you for your selection of this jade. It is wonderful, Qing dynasty perhaps."

I wanted to imply that it was my present to her, but of course the pendant was company paid and a cost of doing business with Ashraf. "It was my distinct pleasure to be helpful."

I reached for a topic that would draw me closer to her but fell clumsily short. "Have you ever thought about traveling abroad, to the states perhaps?"

Her lips were closed but the corners drew up just enough to make a smile. She knew her effect on men but didn't abuse it.

"I have too much to occupy myself with here."

I reached again. "Did you go to university in Malaysia?"

She studied me for a long second. "My parents have a food stall in Jalan Sayur. There was barely enough money to educate my brothers."

"But you're so knowledgeable."

"I can read, Frederick. In three languages."

Ashraf reappeared before I could trip over myself again. Dinner conversation was politically and socially safe, but Maili kept it from being boring. She could find the interesting core of mundane subjects. I was reminded of a talented Geisha, able to put her men companions at ease.

Ashraf as a Muslim did not drink alcohol, and Maili never drank in his presence. As we ate Maili kept her eyes on Ashraf, glancing occasionally at me. I spent the evening nursing a glass of wine and trying not to stare at her. When we'd finished, Ashraf didn't help Maili up from the table, and they left the restaurant side by side, still not touching. It struck me that I had never seen them in physical contact.

The next morning I flew on to Singapore, and three days later to New York. Two weeks after getting back I was given a promotion and changed responsibilities. I would no longer be able to travel to southeast Asia on an expense account. I turned my portfolio over to another international sales type with an almost complete briefing. Almost. I neglected to mention the contraband I brought in at Ashraf's request. That relationship was his to develop.

Despite the hurly-burly of new markets and problems, Maili held in focus. Not carnally but as an objet d'art I was deprived of viewing. Three years passed, and she would still, like Venus, sometimes emerge on an oyster shell from the swells of my mind.

And then the sales manager for southeast Asia told me that Ashraf had died. Cancer, he said. And painful. Our business relationship died away with Ashraf. I proposed to our God-level management that I be sent back in to try and resurrect the business, but even I knew that their new executive in Malaysia had his relationships already in place, and my suggestion was declined.

I obtained the names and addresses of Ashraf's two wives and send them condolences and small gifts. But Maili was lost. My brief times with her had been without record or evidence. I didn't know her family name or phone number or email or address. There was no listing in Kuala Lumpur for a studio specializing in Tai Chi and Pilates, and there are thousands of Maili's in Malaysia and Singapore.

Without Ashraf's support her studio could have folded, sending her back to the family food stall for which I had no name. The ambiguity leaves a void for which I have no good description. Maili still occasionally resurfaces for me, and I always wonder if she'd had to sell the jade pendant.

David Carrillo

Harvest of the Bittersweet Plums

The Ford Explorer drove itself to Willows. Daniel did not see the horn-shaped butte rising above the eastern horizon or the bugs splattering across the windshield. There were long stretches of road and towns he did not recall passing. He was too busy arguing with people not actually in the car with him.

The parcel for delivery wasn't ready at the Distribution Center. When the Loading Dock finally produced it, Liz in Dispatch took another 20 minutes to update the barcode.

"You people ought to get your act together," he told her.

"You better stop wagging your finger at me," she answered back. "Who do you think you are?"

She shot a glare full of animosity, and Daniel took a step back. It wasn't a full retreat, but he thought it wise to get out of arm's reach if things got violent.

"Yeah, well—I've got an unhappy customer in Willows. And the fuckups on the loading dock cost me precious time."

It was too early to have Liz in his face. But what galled him most, the encounter need not have happened at all. If his wife, Leanne, had only rolled over and gone back to sleep, he would not have reported to work that morning.

"For goodness sakes, who is calling on a Sunday?" he remembered her saying.

Daniel couldn't have cared less. He punched "decline" on the mobile phone and sent it bouncing across the carpet. Daniel wasn't religious or anything, but Sunday was his day off.

The damn thing rang again.

"Dan—neee. It's six thir—teee."

"Don't worry about it."

"If you don't answer it, they'll call the house and wake the kids."

Daniel flung off the comforter on his side of the bed to retrieve the phone from its landing spot and stomped into the bathroom to identify the caller. Standing over the commode, he swiped. It was work. Daniel listened to the voicemail. An overnight package on Friday did not make the truck, and there was a complaint. The Weekend Manager wanted him to handle it.

"Son of a bitch. Not today," he said to the bathroom wall.

Daniel shook himself, pulled up his boxers, and went into the kitchen to turn on the coffeemaker. Leaning against the Formica counter, he retrieved the email detailing the customer's name and location. Daniel still was proving himself at "Bring It Express." He wanted to advance in the company, but he was still on the bubble, showing his bosses they chose the right guy. Handling the call would be a feather in his cap.

When Daniel arrived at the Distribution Center, the door to the Business Office was locked, and the Weekend Manager was nowhere to be found. "Somebody's gonna get an earful about this," he told

Liz.

But, it wasn't going to be Liz, and she told him so. "You've got no right, talking to me like that. I've seen mouthy little pipsqueaks like you come and go."

Liz gave Daniel the same red-faced scowl he got from Leanne just an hour and a half before. Everybody was on his case that morning.

"I can't believe you have to work today. It's Sissy's birthday," Leanne said. She didn't have to remind Daniel of that. He knew it was his daughter's birthday. It was Leanne who insisted he answer the call; she now forfeited the right to complain about it.

The muscles tightened around his mouth. "I'm going in. And that's all there is to it."

"It's that important?"

"To the customer, it is."

"Where do you have to go?"

"Willows, about 40 miles north of Arbuckle."

"Way up there?"

He wasn't taking the bait. Daniel knew what she was getting at. Leanne questioned how much gas he'd burn. A delivery van was not at his disposal for weekend calls. He'd have to take the family's car and get reimbursed for mileage later.

"I told you not to worry about it."

Daniel flicked on the light switch in the bedroom. Leanne sat up in bed, shading her eyes. He yanked a shirt and pair of slacks from hangers in the closet.

"But we have chairs to pick up and the cake," she said. "How am I supposed to get the kids to the bowling alley?"

"How?" It wasn't that he didn't care. Daniel could not allow her to talk him out of doing what he had to do. It was his bread and butter. The company motto was "We Do What It Takes." Leanne didn't understand that. To her, family always came first. It was chicken-shit, walking away from his family like that. He knew it. But what else could he do?

"I don't understand why you are so angry all the time," Leanne said. "I don't know what I'm going to do now."

He couldn't handle the disappointment in her voice. Determined to have the last word, Daniel growled back. "It's a goddamn paycheck, all right? It's what pays the bills around here. You'll just have to make do."

"Ha!" he said while driving up Interstate Highway 505. Daniel recollected how he had set his wife straight before leaving the house. Although he derived satisfaction from winning the argument at home, the quarrel ran contrary to the mindset he needed for the job. If he was incapable of soothing his spouse's grievances, how in the world was he going to finesse an unhappy customer in Willows? Then, boom! Daniel hit the brakes.

The Explorer swerved onto the soft median to avoid a rear-end collision with the Mazda ahead. He hadn't noticed that traffic had slowed to a crawl. Knight Motor Transport and Matheson Fast Freight had both lanes of the interstate jammed. He could not see his way around the big semis that boxed him in. So, Daniel got off at the next exit and stopped at the Taco Bell in Williams. Valuable time lost, it was now 10:21. He would never make it back in time for cake and ice cream. Daniel guzzled down a large Pepsi and stopped in the john to take a lengthy whiz.

Customer service was a thankless job. His

supervisor, Rita, likened it to being eaten alive. "You either cut your way out of the bowels or end up a pile of shit," she said. To Liz, in Dispatch, Daniel was already a piece of shit. She would make a big stink to management about him pointing his finger in her face.

Daniel remembered how she stood at the counter with big, surly eyes. "Well, maybe, Liz, if you'd–" He was ready to say something really nasty but stopped short. "Let me do my goddamn job."

Daniel grabbed the errant package and stormed out into the parking lot before realizing that he left a hundred-dollar pair of Ray-bans sitting on the counter. Liz could keep them for all he cared. Daniel could not stomach another minute of her snarky attitude.

Rehashing the morning's events sent him spinning. Daniel cringed and shouted aloud, swerving into the next lane. The Prius next to him slowed to create plenty of space for the madman up ahead. In the rearview mirror, Daniel could see the horror on the woman driver's face—as if he intended to run her fuel-efficient vehicle off the road. It was his life that recklessly ran off the road.

What kind of father wakes his daughter to wish her a happy birthday only to say goodbye? I hope you like your presents, sorry I won't be here when you open them. Being on-call 24/7 sucked. *How do you explain to a seven-year-old the crappy choices adults have to make? Kids see through the bullshit.* There was no excuse for him to be anywhere else but home: blowing up balloons and barbecuing hot dogs. "Don't worry," he reassured her. "I'll be home in time for cake and ice cream.

—

Willows is a "two exit town." If Daniel missed the exit, he'd have to drive all the way to Oroville before he could turn around. He didn't have time for that, so he kept a careful watch on the road signs. Like so many little towns, Willows is barely visible off I-5—no landmarks, just stacked bales of hay and big sky all around. A yellow bi-plane dusted the amber fields by the highway. The GPS directions were: "In 4.3 miles, take Exit 608." He made the turnoff at 11:06.

The main drag was fast food joints, rundown motels, and old houses converted into chiropractor offices. The parking lot at Saint Monica's Church was full. The upstanding people of Willows turned out to hear the "good word" at Sunday's mass. He passed the cemetery on the outskirts of town—with its tall obelisks, mausoleums, and magnificent sculptures—where the fine citizens would go to their final resting place. *How convenient*, he thought, *such a short journey*.

The GPS chimed in again: "Turn left onto Country Road 99 and go 0.3 miles to Road 48." He was in the country now—agricultural land on both sides of the frontage road, to the right, a wet rice crop. On the south side, a sprawling orchard. Rays of sunshine illuminated sapphire-colored fruit decorating the green-leafed branches. Brown faces beneath faded baseball caps huddled together, taking a water break from picking fruit.

Daniel's mobile phone rang. "Did you get lost, Acosta?" It was 11:21, and the delivery wasn't registered in the scanner yet.

"No, I'm not lost."

He'd be halfway home by now if management hadn't dropped the ball, and the package was ready to go. Daniel was tempted to tell the son of a bitch off, but the GPS interjected: "Veer left at Road 47 in one-tenth of a mile."

"I'm five minutes away."

"I better not get another call from Mrs. Miyamoto telling me you haven't arrived yet," the hot-headed manager said.

The son of a bitch was still carping at Daniel when he rolled down the car window. The mosquito splattered windshield made it difficult to see the road. He missed the Ray-bans he left behind at the Distribution Center. The polarized lenses would have cut through the glare. Daniel stuck his face outside of the driver's side window to get a better look. An oncoming car had wandered into his lane—a Saab on a collision course—growing larger every second. Daniel froze behind the wheel. The panicked face of a young dark-haired woman gaped back. Daniel swerved into the oncoming lane in the nick of time to avoid hitting the sedan.

But fate or divine providence put another vehicle at the junction that morning—a green pickup truck. Daniel yanked hard on the steering wheel to miss the old clunker flashing by. The Ford Explorer careened across the road toward the irrigation ditch. At the last moment, it fishtailed, sending it in the opposite direction.

Daniel sailed through an orchard, branches whipping across the windshield. Dirt clods pelted the bottom of the car before it slid into a tree. The seat belt stopped him from hitting the steering wheel. The force of the airbag slammed hard into his face and chest. Daniel stared into a powdery white cloud. A muffled voice said, "Acosta. Acosta? Are you there?" The phone had landed somewhere on the floorboard.

The Reverend Kneale and his wife Emma were on their way to visit sick parishioners at Glenn Medical Center. Their green Dodge pickup had a near-miss on Road 47 with a red Ford traveling in the opposite direction. The retired pastor hurried through the orchard in his Sunday best to assist the other driver. A glassy-eyed man squeezed out of the SUV, struggling to put one foot in front of the other. The American Country Countdown boomed from his car radio.

"You all right, young fella?"

The thirty-something driver dropped his mobile phone before rolling an ankle.

"Look here, you'd better let me help," Kneale said, quick to sit the injured man down against a tree.

"What's your name?"

The young man didn't seem to comprehend what Rev. Kneale had asked. The company logo embroidered on his shirt indicated that he worked for a courier service. He was bleeding from cuts on his forehead and nose, and there was swelling under his right eye.

Rev. Kneale gave the handkerchief from the breast pocket of his suit jacket to the injured man so he could wipe the blood from his face.

"Did I? Is she?"

"You nearly collided with the missus and me."

The courier seemed incapable of stringing more than a couple of words together. So, the Reverend carried on the conversation for both of them.

"My wife, Emma, is attending to the other driver," he said. "I haven't the foggiest idea of why she wandered into your lane."

The courier stared up at the green canopy, heavy with fruit.

"I see you are admiring Willow's world-famous plums," the Reverend said.

He plucked a low hanging plum from a lower branch to examine it. "This one is a real dandy."

The courier considered the purplish-black fruit with a gleam in his eyes. Or maybe they looked glassy due to shock from the accident. The Reverend didn't know for sure.

"Let's get you fixed up," he said, grabbing the young man's elbow and helping him to his feet. Ever the boy scout, the Reverend had a first aid kit under the seat of his truck. He steered the injured man through the orchard with slow, steady steps.

When they reached the road, they found Emma struggling to keep a hysterical woman from collapsing. The distraught woman's hair and clothing were dripping wet. Mascara ran down her cheeks.

"Now, now," Emma said. "Everything's going to be all right."

"My girl, my girl," the woman cried. "I need to go to her."

"Let's tend to you first. And then we'll go."

The young woman fought to get away. It was all Emma and her husband could do to keep her from running across Road 47 toward the canal. The couple's gentle assurances finally coaxed the distraught mother into the passenger seat of the Dodge pickup.

Meanwhile, the courier wandered across the road to where it branched off into Road 48. He followed the single lane to where it crossed over to the canal and studied the break in the viaduct's flat water.

"Call 911," he shouted.

"Dear God in Heaven," the Reverend said, comprehending the situation, "I guess, I'd better."

Daniel crossed the road to where a set of deep cut tire track displaced the gravel on the shoulder. He spotted a glossy, rainbow streak on the surface of the water in the irrigation ditch. A warning on a sign posted on the access road read: "Absolutely No Swimming or Jumping from the Bridge."

The self-doubt rattling around his brain ceased. No longer did he suffer the pain of his injuries. Daniel did what any compassionate person would do in that situation. He slid down the steep bank through the thick Joe Pye, and dog paddled into the canal. With his face down in the cold water, Daniel searched below. It was too murky to see much, and when he came up for air, Daniel realized the current had pushed him downstream from the spot where he'd seen the tell-tale slick. The weight of his street clothes restricted his movements as he swam against the current.

A kick from his breaststroke struck something below. A detached pink bow swirled by, turning in the flow. Without hesitation, Daniel dove down into the cloudy water. Through the stirred-up silt, he could see a web of diamonds dance upon a metallic rooftop. Daniel grabbed ahold of the Saab's luggage rack.

He noticed the driver-side window a third of the way open. A stream of bubbles drifted through the gap. The distraught mother must have squeezed out here. It was apparent, Daniel would never fit through the narrow space—not without becoming stuck. He pulled at the door handle instead. There was a flicker of movement inside. He wasn't religious or anything, but Daniel said a prayer before giving the door handle another hard tug.

A set of eyes popped out the dark compartment. Long strands of golden hair billowed like water grasses, bending with the current. Daniel pushed away from the car and swam up for air. When he surfaced, an explosion of wings beat against the shattered sky. Choking on swallowed water, Daniel struggled to keep afloat. A set of strong hands grabbed his collar. Through the ensnaring water reeds, a broad-shouldered rancher with a determined jaw pulled him to safety.

"There's a girl down there," Daniel said, gasping for air. His broken thoughts kept him from saying more. But the rancher understood.

"We'll take it from here," he said.

Migrant field hands climbed down the embankment, ready to assist in the rescue effort. White fluff from Joe Pye weeds danced upon the breeze—rising and then falling again, lifeless upon the moving water.

Daniel climbed onto broken concrete slabs near the bridge. The cool breeze against his wet skin gave him goosebumps. Sharp, stabbing pains in his chest made him wince. The farmhands helped Daniel to the road, slow and easy. "Dejanos ayudarte," one said.

It was after dark when Daniel got home. In front, abandoned at the curb, was a strange burned-out car. *Who left this here?* Walking up the driveway, he wondered if Leanne knew anything about it. The front door was locked, and he didn't have the key. Daniel rang the doorbell, but no one answered. He could hear laughter coming from inside. Daniel saw his Aunt Rachel in the living room, talking to Mike. It was strange to see him there because Mike and Daniel weren't exactly on friendly terms. Mike lived on the corner. He drove too fast down the street when the

Acosta children were out playing. Heated words had been exchanged, and Daniel let the air out of his tires.

He went around the side of the house to look inside the kitchen window. The open refrigerator door illuminated Leanne's face. No matter how much he tapped at the window, she did not notice him there. Leanne poured punch from a pitcher into Dixie cups, placing them on a tray. She chatted with Mrs. Miyamoto, the Bring It Express customer from Willows who could not wait until Monday.

He went into the backyard to try the sliding glass door. Family and friends were gathered in the den decorated with balloons and streamers. Leanne passed out the punch, assisted by Mrs. Miyamoto, while Sissy and Dee and twelve little tadpoles darted about. Birthday presents were stacked on a folding table in the center of the room. Sissy picked up a gift. But instead of opening it, she handed her present to a girl wearing a "Sleeping Beauty" gown. Little Briar Rose had flowing blond hair and gray-green eyes.

"Sissy. No," Daniel said, tugging at the door latch.

The princess held Daniel in her gaze, seeing him when nobody else could.

"Danny? Dan—neee?"

He was fidgeting with the IV tubes taped to his forearms.

"No, hon, it's your pain medication," Leanne told him.

Danny's upper lip curled in irritation as he pulled at the uncomfortable tubes. The male nurse rushed in to stop him. The nurse was pleasant enough, but he tethered Daniel's wrists to the guardrails before resetting the equipment.

"You have a broken sternum, Danny. Lay still."

"Do I got a choice?" he snapped, unable to free his wrists.

Danny lay helpless in the small windowless room with its constant beeping noises, propped up on the raised hospital bed. Every movement hurt, no matter how slight. His face contorted in the half-light. A purplish-black swelling closed his right eye.

"What time is it?" he asked.

"It's after 8:00," Leanne said, glancing at her watch. "I can only stay awhile longer. I still need to check-in at the Travelodge. Dee and Sissy are hungry."

"Sissy and Dee?" Daniel sat up. "They're here?"

"In the waiting room with Susan."

"She's here?"

Leanne had once confided to Susan that she and Danny had marriage troubles. She told Susan how he called her a "fat pig" and ridiculed her for not bringing in enough income from her manicuring business. Susan called Danny an "asshole" at a backyard barbecue for saying mean things to Leanne. She appreciated Susan standing up for her. Susan was a good friend. Although Daniel didn't care much for her after that.

"Susan was nice enough to come along and help with the kids."

"I want to see her," Danny said.

"Susan?"

"No, Sissy—to ask about her party."

"They don't let the little girls into emergency rooms, silly. She's not old enough."

"Did she have a good birthday?"

"She had a great birthday. All her friends came, and she loved her gifts."

Leanne's assessment of the party left a sad smile

on her husband's face. She knew Danny regretted not being there.

He grimaced while trying to adjust himself in the bed.

"Why are they keeping me here?" Danny asked.

"They've got you under observation, hon."

Daniel groaned.

"They're taking good care of ya, I hope," a voice said with a country drawl. "This town is indebted to Good Samaritans, like you." The retired pastor, Reverend Kneale, stood in the doorway carrying a brown paper bag.

"You're a hero," Leanne said.

Danny shook his head. "No."

The Reverend chuckled. "Well, the Sheriff thinks so."

"How would he know?"

"Dan—neee!"

"Your husband was pretty banged up. And still, he found the gumption to search for the child," the good-natured fellow said.

Danny groaned and shifted in the bed.

"The little girl was trapped inside a car at the bottom of an irrigation ditch," Reverend Kneale continued.

"I'm more or less to blame," Danny said.

"Sssh, Danny," Leanne said, stroking a lock of his hair. "Lay still."

"Wait a doggone minute, son. Don't go beating yourself up. It was an accident. And there was nothing more you could have done. It was in God's hands and in his hands alone."

Daniel recalled watching rescue efforts from the rear gate of the paramedic truck. It hurt when the EMT pushed fingers into his chest. The real hero was the big farmer. He carried the girl from the treacherous canal waters. The farmer cradled her in his arms as if she had fallen asleep there.

"Did they do CPR?"

Reverend Kneale confirmed what Danny already knew. "They did what they could, son."

Danny's eyes rolled back in his head.

The older man smiled back at Danny with soft, understanding eyes. He informed Danny and Leanne that the other driver's name was Miranda. "She turned to fuss at her daughter, Jessica, in the back seat. They were on their way to a birthday party."

Tears zipped down Danny's cheeks. Leanne gathered tissues and leaned over the rail to wipe them. She gazed at her husband's face, trying to comprehend the sorrow that gripped him. His sadness scared her. *Will he be able to find his way back to me and the girls?*

Reverend Kneale squeezed Danny's hand. "I came by to tell you that the Sheriff has delivered your company's package. When Mrs. Miyamoto heard about the accident, she called your boss to express her gratitude.

"Isn't that nice, hon?" Leanne said, beaming.

"Oh, and I forgot to tell you the best part. Sheriff Deputies towed your Ford into town. You're in luck, ma' boy. O'Malley's Auto Repair will have it ready on Tuesday—there was only minor damage to the front end."

Before the old gent left, he handed Leanne a grocery bag full of juicy, fat plums. He told her not to worry, that he and the missus would see to the family's needs while they were in town. Leanne hugged the stoop-shouldered clergyman for his kindness.

Then, the Acosta's were alone again, man and

wife, in the dark emergency room—their faces hidden in shadow. Leanne wanted to say something but was unsure of the right words. When she finally worked up the courage, Leanne leaned forward into the light beaming in through the door.

"I was cranky this morning. I know you had to go to work. I was just disappointed you weren't going to be with us. But everything worked out. As it turned out, you were needed here in Willows to help that poor girl."

"No, you were right this morning. I should have stayed home."

"It's like Rev. Kneale said, Danny, you can't change what happened. Sometimes you got to leave it up to God. You know, hon?"

Danny stared into the empty hallway, where the Reverend had departed. He seemed deep in thought and melancholy. Leanne was about to kiss Danny goodnight and take the girls to the Travelodge when his eyes refocused again.

Danny wanted something to eat. He asked Leanne if she could get the nurse.

"Why don't you have one of these plums the Reverend brought?"

Leanne untethered one of Danny's arms from the railing and handed him two black, short-stemmed plums. They were ripe and ready to eat. Daniel offered one of the plums to Leanne to sample.

"No, thank you."

Danny proceeded to take a bite out of the beat red flesh. The juice squirted on his face, running down his neck, and splattering on the front of his hospital gown. The mess did not bother him in the least. It seemed to give him pleasure. He smiled and took another bite into the smooth-skinned fruit.

Leanne wiped the juice from his face with a washcloth. "Goodness gracious, Danny."

"Do you realize these are the best plums in the world?"

Leanne helped Danny change out of the soiled gown and into a fresh one. Danny gazed into her eyes, unsure of where things stood with their relationship, Leanne's eyes darted away.

"Grown right here in Willows," he continued, as if he spoke on behalf of the Chamber of Commerce. "It would be a shame to come all the way up here without trying one."

Waving him off, Leanne said, "I don't care for one, right now."

Danny drew in his cheeks and sucked on the pit before spitting the taupe stone into the tray.

Leanne awaited his ridicule. Danny did not like being told "no." He liked things done his way. When she said or did otherwise, Danny became testy and called her all sorts of mean things.

But this time, he did not parry her refusal with sarcasm or demeaning remarks. Instead, the corners of his mouth inched up into a smile. This put her instantly at ease. There was a lightness of spirit in the room that Leanne found refreshing and reassuring. Daniel's eyes were as soft as a Lutheran Pastor's.

She stopped fussing with his hospital gown and sat at the edge of the bed to try a plum from the bag Rev. Kneale had left. Juice dribbled down her chin as she took a bite. It was delicious. She didn't have to say so. The excitement on her face was enough to let him know that she was free from the memory of how a plum should taste.

"Did I tell you about what happened at the bowling alley today?"

"I don't believe you did."

"Oh, the girls were so cute. Where should I start?"

Leanne had held back before, even though she knew Danny wanted to hear all about Sissy's party. Did she punish him for not being there? Or, was it was leftover resentment from that morning? Whatever the reason, it seemed silly now to hold on to such feelings. Leanne recounted for her husband every detail of her day leading up to their daughter's birthday celebration. It had been years since he shown such interest in what she shared, years since he listened to her so completely.

Chris Viner is a writer based in Los Angeles. He is the author of Lemniscate (nominated for a Pushcart Award). His work appears in Ash, Colorado Review, Critical Read, The Festival Review and The London Magazine, among others. He holds degrees from Goldsmiths, University of London and St Anne's College, University of Oxford, where he was a recipient of the Pasby Prize for his writing.

Kenneth N. Margolin is a retired attorney, and lives with his wife, Judith, in Newton, Massachusetts. As an attorney, Ken made it a sacred mission to avoid legalese in his professional writing. Still relatively new to fiction, Ken's stories have been published in print and online, in Pif Magazine, Evening Street Review, Twenty-Two Twenty-Eight, Short Edition, The Literary Hatchet, among others; poetry in Shot Glass Journal.

Rudolfo San Miguel earned a bachelor's degree in creative writing from San Francisco State University. He has written fiction for ten years and continues to develop as a writer, drafting stories that amuse him. He hopes they amuse you as well.

Norbert Kovacs lives and writes in Hartford, Connecticut. He has published stories in Westview, Thin Air, Headway, Corvus Review, and The Write Launch. His website is www.norbertkovacs.net.

Ed Ahern resumed writing after forty odd years in foreign intelligence and international sales. He's had over three hundred fifty stories and poems published so far, and six books. Ed works the other side of writing at Bewildering Stories, where he sits on the review board and manages a posse of six review editors. www.twitter.com/bottomstripper, www.facebook.com/EdAhern73/?ref=bookmarks, www.instagram.com/edwardahern1860/

David A. Carrillo lives in Benicia, California. Carrillo also writes travel literature and historical fiction. His story "Vengeance Was She" is scheduled to appear in a 2021 issue of Frontier Tale.

Thank you to the Wapshott Press sponsors, supporters, and Friends of the Wapshott Press.

Muna Deriane
Kit Ramage
Rachel Livingston
Thomas Loper
Ann and John Brantingham
David Meischen
John O'Kane
Laurel Sutton
Suzanne Siegel
James and Rebecca White
Robert Earle and Mary Azoy
Ronni Kern
Toni Rodriguez
Steve Misuraca
LindaAnn LoSchiavo
Kathleen Waener
Phil Temples
Richard Whittaker
Alice Frances Wickham

The Wapshott Press is a 501(c)(3) not-for-profit press publishing work by emerging and established authors and artists. We publish books that should be published. We are very grateful to the people who believe in our plans and goals, as well as our hopes and dreams. Our website is at www.WapshottPress.org. Donations gratefully accepted at www.Donate.WapshottPress.org.

www.ingramcontent.com/pod-product-compliance
Lightning Source LLC
Chambersburg PA
CBHW070503130626
46555CB00003B/1136